KT-214-684

'Make love with me tonight.'

Her heart was thumping, her breathing choppy, her lips felt plumped and tender. 'It's crazy,' she said. Because she couldn't say no, even though she knew she should. She shook her head, the pain of that night thirteen years ago refusing to be ignored. 'You had your chance. You threw me out.'

'A long time ago.'

'You hate me.'

'I want you.'

'And I hate *you*!'

'Do you? You didn't kiss me like you hated me.'

Her teeth found one kiss-swollen lip and she raked them over its unfamiliar plumpness. 'One night?'

'Just one night. And then we go our separate ways.'

Trish Morey is an Australian who's also spent time living and working in New Zealand and England. Now she's settled with her husband and four young daughters in a special part of South Australia, surrounded by orchards and bushland, and visited by the occasional koala and kangaroo. With a life-long love of reading, she penned her first book at age eleven, after which life, career and a growing family kept her busy, until once again she could indulge her desire to create characters and stories—this time in romance. Having her work published is a dream come true. Visit Trish at her website, www.trishmorey.com

Recent titles by the same author:

FORCED WIFE, ROYAL LOVE-CHILD
THE ITALIAN BOSS'S MISTRESS OF REVENGE
THE SHEIKH'S CONVENIENT VIRGIN

THE RUTHLESS GREEK'S VIRGIN PRINCESS

BY
TRISH MOREY

◉™ MILLS & BOON®
Pure reading pleasure™

DID YOU PURCHASE THIS BOOK WITHOUT A COVER?

If you did, you should be aware it is **stolen property** as it was reported
unsold and destroyed by a retailer. Neither the author nor the publisher
has received any payment for this book.

All the characters in this book have no existence outside the imagination
of the author, and have no relation whatsoever to anyone bearing the
same name or names. They are not even distantly inspired by any
individual known or unknown to the author, and all the incidents are
pure invention.

All Rights Reserved including the right of reproduction in whole or
in part in any form. This edition is published by arrangement with
Harlequin Enterprises II BV/S.à.r.l. The text of this publication or
any part thereof may not be reproduced or transmitted in any form
or by any means, electronic or mechanical, including photocopying,
recording, storage in an information retrieval system, or otherwise,
without the written permission of the publisher.

This book is sold subject to the condition that it shall not, by way of
trade or otherwise, be lent, resold, hired out or otherwise circulated
without the prior consent of the publisher in any form of binding or
cover other than that in which it is published and without a similar
condition including this condition being imposed on the subsequent
purchaser.

® and TM are trademarks owned and used by the trademark owner
and/or its licensee. Trademarks marked with ® are registered with the
United Kingdom Patent Office and/or the Office for Harmonisation in
the Internal Market and in other countries.

First published in Great Britain 2009
Harlequin Mills & Boon Limited,
Eton House, 18-24 Paradise Road, Richmond, Surrey TW9 1SR

© Trish Morey 2009

ISBN: 978 0 263 87417 4

Set in Times Roman 10½ on 12¾ pt
01-0809-44910

Printed and bound in Spain
by Litografia Rosés, S.A., Barcelona

THE RUTHLESS GREEK'S VIRGIN PRINCESS

For darling Kate, whose strength of spirit
and sense of humour knows no bounds and who is
an inspiration to us all (and who demanded from her
sickbed to know why it took me so long to dedicate a
book to her, so I just had to do it again☺),

for Eleni, to whom I am eternally grateful, *efharisto*,

and for the fabulous Maytoners, whose friendship,
laughter and wisdom are like a lifeline.
Thank you for keeping me sane.

Love you all heaps.

Trish

x

PROLOGUE

Paris

THERE was thunder in his head, a foul taste in his mouth and a naked woman in his bed, the latter almost enough to make him forget everything else. She was smooth, her bare skin like silk and satin under hands that felt too clumsy and unresponsive for his wants. Her small, nimble hands soothed his frustration, firing his anticipation with clever fingers that seemed to track the need under his skin while her mouth set fire to other places—the angle of his jaw, the jut of his collarbone, and below.

He reached for her with leaden arms still heavy with alcohol and sleep, but she just laughed, wicked and low, and slipped out of his grasp, and it was too dark to see, so he collapsed back into the pillows, the blur in his head turning jagged and sharp as he tried to make sense of things. But there was no thinking, not with her attacking from a different direction, her mouth a circle of fire on the inside of one knee, her tongue the brand of a torch on the bare skin of his thigh.

The sensations split cracks in the pain in his head, tiny fissures that memories squeezed through, blowing into life. Memories of arriving in Paris at his father's command, of his father shouting, of him arguing back, and of the gut-wrenching blow when he'd realised that he had no choice…

His tongue felt thick, his mouth dry, and the unfamiliar taste of stale whisky clung thick on his breath. How much had he drunk?

Blood thundered in his ears, drumming in a skull that seemed to ache more with every beat, a beat that pushed his blood south until another part of him throbbed and kicked. Then her two small hands were around him, and the breath was punched from his lungs. Cool hands. Smooth hands. Bewitching hands.

And then, just when he thought he could take no more, she flicked his very tip with her tongue. Just a graze, and yet still he bucked underneath her as if he'd been hit with a bolt of electricity, swelling even more and forcing her hands to loosen their grip.

He reached a hand to his pounding head, sure his skull must be swelling with each hammer blow. Was this their fathers' idea? To seal the deal? So that there was no going back?

From the putrid depths of a drink-addled brain, anything seemed possible. They'd both been vehement that the engagement would go ahead. So they'd sent Elena here, naked to his bed, to seduce him and maybe create the child that would mean there was no chance of escape, no chance of avoiding the fate his father had carved out for him.

He rubbed his aching, slick brow with one hand, wishing he could think clearly, wishing away the fog that filled his brain, but sick with the knowledge that it could indeed be true. After tonight he knew their fathers were capable of anything. His fate was sealed. There was no going back.

And then she straddled him, one hand still on him, and he pulled away his arm and opened his eyes again, battling the pain that shot through his brow as his eyes struggled to focus in the dark.

She moved over him, guiding him past the brush of curls to her entrance, and heat flared again as she brought him to that slick sweet spot, only to have rebellion course through his brain in a vivid flash of pain. Even if there was nothing he could do about this marriage, he would not be taken like some prize of war! If anyone did the pillaging around here, it would be him. And she would know it!

With a roar that thundered in his head like cannon fire, he surged up, catching her in his arms and rolling her beneath him before her cry of surprise had faded away. His head was thumping with the sudden movement, his gut rebelling, but he had more important things on his mind. Still, just for a moment he allowed his hands to sweep up her sweet body. This time, trapped beneath him, she would not get away. He caught her breasts, smaller than he'd expected, but it wouldn't be the first time the reality had failed to match up with the promotion. Besides, they were firm and peaked, and in the fog of his brain, he wasn't about to complain. Not when they were the best things he'd felt all night. And if he could feel anything through the war zone that was his head, he'd take it.

Even so, he would make her pay for playing this part in their fathers' sordid business deal. He dipped his head and took her tightly budded breast into his mouth. Her body arched beneath him, and she shuddered as his hand grasped the other breast and squeezed it tight, his teeth grazing her nipple, nipping at her flesh, each nip feeding his anger.

How dared she try to trap him? He'd agreed to marry her, hadn't he? A fire burned inside him, flames fuelled by whisky and want and need and a firm-fleshed woman who had strayed where she shouldn't. He had given their fathers his word. Damn her, he would make her pay!

Through a fog-thick brain and the thump of blood, he heard her cry out, worked out the reason why, and finally released the breast clamped so tightly between his clenched teeth that it was a wonder he hadn't drawn blood. Instantly she relaxed under him, and he laved the rest of her tension away, nuzzling, sucking, until once again she curled like a kitten around him, her silken legs wound around his in an age-old invitation.

He was done with toying with her. She was ready, he knew, so he drew back, his thumb making lazy circles around the screaming tight bud of nerves that had her groaning in pleasure as he positioned himself at her tight entrance.

Another surprise. Elena had struck him as a woman

of the world. Four years his elder, she'd had her share of lovers, he knew that beyond doubt. And yet...

He pushed against flesh slick and yet strangely unwilling and felt her tense beneath him, sensed her holding her breath.

She couldn't be. He was just drunk and clumsy and this time...

And then he heard her cry out, and some familiar but unexpected quality in her voice made his blood run cold. He pulled away, fighting a body screaming for release, a head protesting every jarring movement, his hands scrabbling wildly for a switch he knew was here somewhere. Light erupted in the room and exploded in his head, spears of agony lancing his eyes that he had no choice but to ignore if he were to discover what he feared was true.

And then he turned, and the agony in his head was the least of his worries. Marietta Lombardi, the teenaged sister of his best friend, lay naked in his bed, her eyes wide open and afraid like a rabbit caught in a spotlight, her long blonde hair tangled about her head, her milky-skinned limbs squirming uncomfortably upon the bedlinen.

'What the hell are you doing here?' Each word crashed around his head like a shotgun blast. The effect they had on her was more devastating. She looked mortally wounded as she shrank back against the headboard of the bed, bringing her knees up and clutching her arms about her.

'I wanted to give you something.' Her bottom lip quivered, a bottom lip he'd often been tempted to kiss, although he never had, and now never would. 'I came to give you…me.'

'*No!*' he roared, rising from the bed, dragging the damask cover with him to cover his nakedness until he could reach his robe. She was his best friend's little sister. She was a virgin. And while he'd thought that maybe one day in the future… But there was no chance of that now. No chance of that ever! Not after tonight. 'What the hell were you thinking?'

'I was thinking I wanted to be your birthday present.'

There it was again, the telltale tremble of her bottom lip. And there, on her breast he saw it, the mark of his teeth where he'd bitten her in his anger, and the sight of those red marks on her perfect skin sent pain slicing through him anew. Oh, God, this was wrong, on so many levels. He'd been about to take her, to bury himself into her, to punish her as if she'd done him wrong.

And he'd hurt her.

He raked his hands through his hair.

'You have to go.'

'But… Yannis.'

'You have to go!'

'You were going to make love to me. You were. Why can't you. Why did you stop?'

He growled into the room. 'Because I didn't know who you were then!'

'So who did you think I was?' She had the nerve to look incensed, and he almost laughed. Almost. Because there was nothing funny about it.

'Just…get out of here.'

'But I love you.'

'You're sixteen. You can't love me.'

'But you love me. You told me!'

He stormed away again, his fists hard against his brow, fighting the agony inside, fighting the injustice and the foolishness that comes with recalling a day filled with green fields and daisy chains and blue skies and a girl who had always seemed perfect for him.

He felt her hand on his shoulder and wheeled around. She was naked and trembling, her creamy skin goose-bumped, her rose-pink nipples pebbled and hard. She took his hand and placed it over one breast, so that the hard nipple jutted into his palm and his fingers curled into her firm flesh, making his body jerk once again into life.

'I want you,' she said, with a brazenness he'd never seen in her before, twin slashes of red staining her cheeks, a brazenness that had her reaching out for the place where he lay swelling beneath. 'Please make love to me.'

Sto thiavolo, but he was tempted. She moved herself closer into him, taking his silence for assent, pressing her breasts into his chest, her mouth suckling at his flesh while a new agony played out in his aching mind.

He could take her now, and nobody need ever know. Nobody would be any the wiser. One night of perfection before he married Elena. Was it too much to ask?

He wove his fingers through the curtain of her hair, wound its weight around his thumbs, pressing his lips to her hair, already sinking. And she looked up at him with such a look of adoration in her eyes, such a look of love and trust, that he felt sickened he'd even considered it. How could he do that to Marietta—bed her one night and declare his engagement to another the next?

It couldn't happen.

It couldn't be allowed to happen.

Not now.

Not ever!

'Get out,' he told her, unwinding her arms from his body and pushing her away. Pushing temptation away. 'I don't want you here.'

Confusion lit her features. 'You don't mean that.'

'Cover yourself up and get out!'

'But I love you. And you love me.'

'Like a sister!' he blurted, the lie coming with the knowledge that a clean break might be cruel, but it was the only way. 'Don't you understand? I love you like a sister. *Nothing* more.'

Her beautiful face crumpled, sudden moisture transforming her eyes to liquid, her cheeks sheeting with tears. 'But you said—'

'It doesn't matter what I said! Don't you understand? I can never love you any other way. Now get out and get back to your room before anyone sees you.'

'But Yannis—'

'*Go!*'

CHAPTER ONE

The Island of Montvelatte—thirteen years later

HE WAS close, she could feel it.

It wasn't just the prickle at the base of her neck and the catch in her throat that had Marietta Lombardi on full alert. It was the way the air seemed suddenly thinner, tighter, as if the myriad candles in the Castello's enormous dining room had consumed every last drop of oxygen from the atmosphere, leaving a vacuum that ached to be filled.

And then across the room the ancient timber doors swung open, and even the air in her lungs was sucked out.

Yannis Markides, the man she'd vowed never to see again, was finally here in Montvelatte. Dressed entirely in black, he filled the wide entrance like a dark cloud, his eyes purposefully scanning the throng assembled for the wedding rehearsal dinner while an adrenaline-fuelled wave crashed over her, pinning her to the chair and threatening to free thirteen-year-old memories that had been buried in the deepest recesses of her mind.

Apparently not deeply enough.

Yet even a flood of unwanted memories was no match for seeing him in person. The Yannis of her unbidden and unwanted dreams couldn't hold a candle to this man, who looked more like a warrior about to go into battle than an old family friend. Had he always been so tall? Had he always been able to fill a space with his mere presence? And, in spite of the war-like stance, had he always looked so damned good?

She swallowed down on a sudden lump in her throat. *She didn't need him to look good.* Didn't want him to. She should go now. Slip out in the confusion of waiters serving a multitude of meals before he saw her, before she had to face him again and relive the humiliation of their last encounter.

And then her brother jumped to his feet beside her, calling across the room, and Marietta knew she'd left it too late. The obsidian eyes she'd been hoping to avoid found their mark as they zeroed in on Rafe, his mouth turning into a smile until those same eyes fell on her, lingering so coldly that she shivered, any semblance of a smile frozen clear away, before they snapped back to Rafe so cleanly and decisively as if even looking at her had been a mistake.

Released from his cold-as-a-grave gaze, Marietta felt as if she'd taken a blow to the gut. She'd known Yannis Markides was not the type of man who would forgive and forget, but it was clear he also had no problems holding a grudge. And from the expression on his face as he'd practically seared her with his gaze, he was as unenthusiastic about seeing her as she was about seeing him.

Fine. The sooner this wedding was over, the sooner they could both go back to never seeing each other again, and the happier they'd both be.

So she was here, just as he'd been warned. His fists clenched and unclenched at his sides in time with the thump of his heart, a deep-seated anger turning his vision to red. He'd always believed in the principle that to be forewarned was to be forearmed. The adage had stood him in good stead over the years in both his professional and his private life, and yet now, coming face to face with the woman who'd done more to destroy his family's financial security than any number of corporate sharks he'd had to deal with in his time, the old adage wasn't holding up to scrutiny. Because it wasn't until now that realised the depths of his resentment. It was as if seeing her had rekindled every last spark of anger and bitterness, reigniting old wounds and sending the flames high.

He didn't want to be here, even if it was his best friend's wedding—not if it meant seeing her again, and certainly not if it meant being thrust back into those dark days.

He dragged in a lungful of air heavy with the combined scents of garlic, rosemary and spit-roasted game and sensed something else in the mix—duty. For he had no choice but to be here. One thing he'd learned over the years was that life didn't necessarily serve up what you wanted. He was here, and somehow he was expected to be her opposite number on the bridal party, to be her partner throughout the festivities, even to take her in his arms and dance with her. No amount of forewarning was going to prepare him for that.

He should have brought a woman. He could have had his pick of any number, even after terminating his brief liaison with Susannah, and he cursed the decision that had seen him arrive alone—although he was still sympathetic with the logic of it. Taking a woman to a wedding was fraught with danger. It put ideas in women's heads, ideas that had no place in his relationships.

'Yannis!' She heard her brother's greeting over the chamber music and hubbub of conversation from the assembled guests as the pair met, shaking hands and pulling each other into a man hug before slapping each other on the back. She watched, unable to move, compelled to watch, waiting for the inevitable moment when Rafe would pull Yannis over to introduce him to his bride-to-be, and for the moment when she would have to look him in the eye and greet him and pretend that what had happened thirteen years ago had never taken place.

'So that's Yannis Markides,' Sienna said, leaning across Rafe's empty chair between them, her head still angled towards the reunion between the two men. 'He's very good-looking, isn't he? Almost as good-looking as Rafe.'

Better.

The rogue thought came unbidden and unwelcome, but as much as she tried to clamp down on it, the truth would not be denied. Having inherited the best of their father's genes, her brother was beyond handsome, and in his dress uniform of maroon jacket and ceremonial sash, even more so. But Yannis, with his unique mix of his Montvelattian mother and Greek-Cypriot father, was something else again. It was as if he'd been blessed with the best genes the Mediterranean had to offer, a combination of dark hair, bottomless eyes and chiselled features. As a twenty-one-year-old, he'd been the best-looking man she'd ever seen. Thirteen years on, as a man in his prime, he was utterly arresting.

'I guess so,' she replied at last as she reached for her glass, looking for something tactile and solid and real to cling onto, telling herself he was only a man, a mere mortal like everyone else.

And then she looked up again.

Under the ballroom lighting, his black hair gleamed thick and healthy, his strong features complemented by the play of light and shadow as he moved, with even the angles and planes of his face speaking of nobility.

Mortal? Then why did he have to look so much like a god? Was it any wonder she'd once imagined herself in love with him? What girl wouldn't be naïve enough to let herself imagine, to think that maybe there was something more to it when this man was your brother's best friend and you saw him practically every day of your life, and when he treated you as if you were something special, the way he always had…

What girl wouldn't have made the same mistake she had? She took a deep breath, her fingers locked tight around the stem of her wine glass. Back then she'd been just a teenager, and clearly impressionable at that. Thank God she wasn't so naïve, so easily driven by her hormones any more. And thank God this ordeal would soon be over. A day, maybe two, and the wedding and the associated formalities would be done with, and they would both be gone from the island.

She could hardly wait.

'I can see why he's so popular with the women,' Sienna continued, 'although I can't believe he's alone now. I expected he'd bring a partner.'

Marietta didn't care. Yannis had a reputation as a playboy, the same label her brother had boasted until his world had connected with Sienna's. If Yannis was by himself, she had no doubt it would only be a temporary situation. 'Maybe she saw sense,' she muttered, not quietly enough.

The other woman's head swung around, 'You don't like him? I thought you guys grew up together, one big happy family. At least, that's how Rafe makes it sound.'

Marietta shrugged and forced a smile to her face. 'You know how it is, two's company, three's a crowd. They've always been best friends and I've always been Rafe's little sister.'

Whether she'd placed too much emphasis on the last two words, or whether they'd contained a hint of bitterness that she'd never quite dispelled, Sienna studied her for a second, as if weighing up her answer. Then she nodded and reached over to squeeze her free hand. 'I think I understand.' And Marietta felt a surge of affection for the Australian woman who would soon be her sister-in-law.

The two men turned then, Rafe gesturing towards the women, and something twisted in her gut, pulling her lower into the chair. She let go the glass she was still holding in a rush, lest she tip it over and spill its contents, and battled to dredge up a plastic smile to affix to her face as they came closer.

'You remember Marietta, of course,' her brother said as he led the way, and the dark cloud hovered before her, brooding dangerously over her before she'd had a chance to find her feet, even if she'd been able to remember how to do so, standing so close to her that she dared not attempt the feat now. Not when the look in his eyes damned her to the core, without the merest shred of warmth at meeting her again.

She'd done that, she realised in a rush. She'd banished every good memory he might have of their years together with one foolish and reckless act. And now, just as he had done thirteen years ago, he was still making her pay the price.

So many years later. She'd been a teenager back then. Made just one foolish mistake. Had what she'd done been so unforgivable?

'Yannis,' she said, needing to do something to break the silence that stretched taut like piano wire between them, 'it's been a long time.'

The searing look he sent her in reply told her he thought it nowhere near long enough, before he dipped his head in the barest nod. 'Princess,' he said, and Marietta swallowed. The way he said it made it sound like an insult, but before she could force her tight vocal cords to relax enough to tell him that he could call her Marietta, as he had always done, Rafe had already turned away to introduce his fiancée, and Yannis had severed contact.

Sienna clearly had more presence of mind than Marietta or maybe it was just that the other woman's knees were still working, as she rose from her chair to greet Rafe's lifelong friend, her smile broad and welcoming as he lifted her hand and pressed his lips to the back of it.

'Raphael always insisted he would beat me at everything. At finding the perfect wife, I'm afraid I must concede this contest.'

Sienna laughed a little, her smile widening. 'Rafe told me you were a charmer. I'm surprised you haven't found the woman of your dreams by now.'

Marietta stiffened in her chair as she awaited Yannis's response, although she wasn't entirely sure why. She'd long ago given up the notion that she was the woman of his dreams. Long ago given up caring who he was with. So she topped up her glass of mineral water, needing the distraction and waving away the waiter who had descended upon her ready to do the task himself.

'Yannis will never marry now, I am convinced of that,' Rafe answered for his friend. 'No woman is good enough for him.'

Especially not Marietta. She hadn't even been good enough to sleep with.

Beyond her, Sienna shook her head at her husband-to-be and smiled softly. 'Tell me, Yannis, how is your father now? Rafe said he's been very ill.'

'He has been, although he's thankfully off the critical list. He suffered another stroke a month ago. My mother apologises for not coming to the wedding, but she cannot leave him now.'

'I'm sorry that they can't both be here, but it is so good to meet you at last,' she said. 'Rafe's told me so much about you.'

'None of it good,' Rafe added, urging them all to sit as waiters appeared from nowhere to bring another meal and fill wine and water glasses. Yannis took his place alongside Sienna, and with a sigh of relief Marietta settled in her brother's shadow, happy for the barrier of the grateful couple separating her from their new arrival.

'Although now,' Rafe continued, 'I'll have to take back the bit about not making it to our wedding. You've missed the rehearsal, though. What kept you? You were supposed to be here days ago.'

Yannis shrugged and picked up the large wine glass, swirling the contents and lifting it casually to his nose, and Marietta thought he would never answer, until finally he spoke. 'The US market has been jittery, and with it some of our clients. It seemed unwise to leave too early. As it is, I'll have to head back straight after the wedding.'

Rafe's face darkened, his brow creased. 'You never mentioned jittery clients in your emails.'

'You're getting married,' Yannis countered, 'there are some things you don't need to know. Besides, you have enough on your plate sorting out Montvelatte's finances.'

'Then why not let Kernahan handle it? After all, you hand-picked the new manager yourself. Why couldn't you have left it to him?'

The other man's eyes glowed unnaturally bright as he stared silently out over the crowd, his jawline tight and rigid.

Marietta chose that moment to reach forward for her water, needing to feel something cool in a throat that felt too tight, too dry. In itself it wasn't a foolhardy action. The mistake she made was in turning her head, only to have her eyes connect once again with the man three seats down, who was staring right at her. Sensation sizzled down her spine as the connection was made—and held.

'Oh, I had my reasons,' he muttered, his voice low, his lips tightly drawn, and his eyes still locked on hers so that she was in no doubt that he had waited until the last moment to attend his best friend's wedding so as to avoid her.

Beside her, Rafe made a move to remonstrate, but his fiancée stopped him with one hand on his wrist. 'Rafe, Yannis is here now, in plenty of time for the wedding. That's all that matters.'

And her brother shrugged and let it go, just as Yannis released her eyes so that at last she could drop back in her chair and disappear behind the shield of her brother, her breathing suddenly too shallow and too fast, her pulse racing, as if she'd just run up the Castello's marble staircase.

This was crazy. She should go—tell them she had a headache. It was almost the truth; her nerves were so strung out that she didn't know what she felt other than this decade-plus ache in her bones that just felt plain wrong. She'd plead a headache and go to bed early, and then there would only be the wedding tomorrow and the reception, and then she wouldn't have to see Yannis again. Wouldn't have to sense his near hatred in every look, in every single word.

She'd almost found the courage to stand, had almost found the words she needed to say, when the music suddenly changed tempo, the orchestra switching to a waltz and an air of hushed expectancy falling over the crowd. Her brother beat her to her feet, took his fiancée's hand and pressed his lips to the back of it. 'Come, *cara*, they await the dance.'

'But surely that's after the wedding—at the reception.'

'Not all of these people—' he waved his hand around the room '—will be able to be here for the reception. Many are villagers who have performed a special task or who will be busy themselves tomorrow, preparing the flowers or working in the kitchens. Tonight is our way of saying a special thank you to them.'

Sienna smiled and nodded. 'Of course. Then we mustn't disappoint them.' She took his hand and stood, and the crowd burst into applause, cheering as Rafe led Sienna to the dance floor and folded his soon-to-be wife—*Montvelatte's soon-to-be Princess*—into his arms. She went as if she belonged there, their bodies moving as one to the music, their eyes on each other, their love a palpable thing.

To love someone so much and to have that love returned… how must that feel? Marietta sighed as she watched them effortlessly glide around the dance floor as one. Now, with the eyes of everyone in the room on them, was her chance to escape. She pushed her chair back, reaching for her purse in the same motion.

'You look different,' came a deep voice from beside her, the words innocent enough yet the tone accusatory. She looked around, surprised that anyone in the room had eyes for anyone but the couple on the dance floor, but then Yannis didn't possess eyes so much as pointed barbs that launched out and impaled her, arresting her escape mid-flight. She swallowed, her back straightening, refusing to be cowed even if her ability to stand had once again deserted her.

'You mean with my clothes on?'

His expression grew darker and harder, and she bit down hard on her bottom lip, wishing she'd managed to form the words in her brain before she'd allowed herself to utter the retort. The look on his face was enough to tell her that the last thing either of them needed was a reminder of that night.

But what did he expect? His attitude had hardly been conciliatory from the moment he'd walked into the room and his gaze had first connected with hers. Why shouldn't she go on the attack when he obviously needed to realise how ridiculous his petty grudge really was?

'I meant you looked older,' he growled once he'd recovered.

Of course that was what he'd meant.

She forced a smile to her lips, but there was no forcing it any further than that. 'Did you? That sounds so much better, thank you.'

'You know what I meant,' he snarled

'It has been thirteen years. Is it any surprise I've

grown up a bit since then?' Out on the dance floor the Prince and his bride-to-be spun together, two halves of a whole, totally absorbed in each other, totally oblivious to whatever tension existed beyond their world. Marietta watched their effortless glide with an envious eye.

'Have you?'

She looked back at him, the vision of her brother and his wife making her lose her train of thought. 'Have I what?'

'Grown up.'

She dragged in a breath, oxygen destined to fuel the fire already burning inside her. 'People change with time, Yannis. Maybe you should try it one day.' There was no point staying any longer. She stood, determined this time to leave. It would be easier this way. She wouldn't have to plead a headache. Yannis wouldn't require any explanation at all. He'd just be happy she was gone.

But Yannis was standing, too, and blocking her way. 'Where do you think you're going?'

'I'm leaving.'

'You can't leave yet.'

He had to be kidding. 'I'm sorry, but I'll do whatever I damn well like. So if you wouldn't mind getting out of my way?'

'It's Rafe and Sienna's rehearsal dinner.'

Now her breathing was more impatient than ever. 'Don't you think I know that? I was here for it, remember? I'm not the one who blew in late.'

A muscle tightened in his jaw. His eyes grew hard and even colder. 'Maybe not, but that doesn't mean you can avoid your responsibilities now.' He gestured towards the dance floor. 'Your brother clearly expects us to join them.' He extended a reluctant arm to her. 'Shall we?'

She blinked up at him, her head already moving into a shake. 'You must be mad.'

And then he nodded in the direction of the dancing couple, and she followed his gaze to where Rafe was spinning his wife-to-be around the dance floor. 'We are expected to join them.'

A lump lodged in her throat, and she swallowed, trying to shift it. He expected her to dance with him? To be escorted around the dance floor in those arms tonight? *No way.* It was one thing to be expected to do it at the formal reception, but there wasn't a snowball's chance in hell that she would do it tonight. She didn't have the stomach for it. 'I'm sorry,' she said, clutching at her earlier excuse. 'I'm afraid I have a blinder of a headache. I really have to go.'

One dark eyebrow arched as he frowned, disapproval and something else skating across his eyes. 'You're afraid.'

She stiffened at the accusation, resenting the challenge, resenting even more the glimmer of truth his words contained. 'Afraid you'll make my headache worse?' she answered, twisting his words to her own purposes. 'Oh, I'll admit there's every chance of that.'

A muscle in his jaw twitched. 'I'm sure you can tolerate the inconvenience if I can.' His words sounded like gravel on gravel, scraping away at the scars left all those years ago until the flesh was raw and tender and she could almost taste the blood seeping fresh from the wound. 'And don't think I would ask you if I didn't have to, but others are waiting for us before they can dance, so tell me, are you coming willingly, or do I have to drag you to the dance floor?'

So he wanted to dance with her as much as she wanted to dance with him. She wanted the time to roll that thought around her mind, to find out why the concept wasn't as satisfying as it should be. But there was no time because he was right—heads were turned, people were watching them expectantly, waiting for them to join the happy couple. She looked back at him, to the dark-as-night eyes that now held an 'I told you so' glimmer of triumph and she didn't answer, couldn't bring herself to. Instead she just strode past him, her chin held high, not caring if he chose to follow her or not, half wishing he wouldn't so that in spite of the audience waiting, she could just keep walking.

He followed her. She didn't need to turn around to know he was right behind her. She could sense his proximity, feel the heat generated by the man just as surely as she could feel the tide of her sapphire silk gown swirling around her ankles as she strode purposefully towards the dance floor.

She'd barely reached it when he captured one hand and swung her around so firmly that she collided hard against the wall of his chest, knocking the air from her lungs and the sense from her mind. He held onto her with a vice-like grip as if certain she would flee at any moment. 'Dance,' he ordered when she'd stood rigid too long, his legs forcing hers to follow suit, though protesting and awkward.

She didn't want him so close, didn't want to feel the press of his thigh or the heat of his chest. Didn't want her hand wrapped so securely in his long, warm fingers, fingers that had come so close to taking her to paradise so many years ago…

Lost in the echo of sensations long gone, she stumbled, only to be abruptly righted by the man in front of her. And it occurred to her how different a picture their entrance on to the dance floor must look, forced and stiff and unnatural after Rafe and Sienna's silken-smooth coupling.

She mangled still more steps before they managed to find some kind of uncomfortable rhythm. Uncomfortable to Marietta, anyway. There was no telling what Yannis thought or felt beyond his overwhelming aura of resentment.

'Well, this is fun,' she blurted, hating every second of it, resenting the grip he had on her hand and the feel of his large hand in the small of her back. Just being close to him was enough to set her skin on fire with awareness. Having to tolerate his touch—the touch of a man who hated her and made no effort to hide it—was too much to endure.

'Nobody said it would be fun.'

He spun her around as easily as if she were made of balsa wood rather than flesh and blood, using his size to counteract her resistance and make her move with him the way he thought she should.

Exasperated, she took a breath and immediately wished she hadn't, her lungs suddenly full of the scent of the man, the very essence of him captured in one ill-timed gasp for air. She turned her head away, so desperate to find somewhere unpolluted with his scent that she missed yet another step, and their feet collided and clashed. He answered by hauling her even closer so she was plastered from breast downwards against his body, her legs so close to his that she had no choice but to cede to his control. 'What are you doing?' she protested, pushing back her shoulders to try to reclaim some space between them.

'Attempting to look like a couple.'

'We're not a couple.'

'We could at least try to move in the same direction at the same time,' he growled. 'Just dance.'

He didn't say anything after that, and for that she was grateful. So she tried to concentrate on the music and forget all about the way her skin tingled where their bodies met, tried to disregard the warm puff of air that signalled his breath teasing the coils of her hair around her ear. But there was no forgetting the feeling of skin against skin as he held tight to her hand, no ignoring how strong and warm the body plastered next to hers felt. And no amount of music would ever be enough to let her forget exactly who she was dancing with.

So she closed her eyes, wanting to shut off at least one of her senses. It was a mistake, the action just heightening her awareness of him until all she knew was the feel of their bodies swaying together to the music as he expertly guided her around the floor. Somehow, in the midst of flying sparks and backbiting, their bodies had found some kind of synchronicity, and in spite of him being the last person in the world she wanted to be with, the way his body moved against hers was intoxicating.

She could feel an underlying tension to his steps as if every movement was a battle, and yet his moves were masterful, long lean legs powering his big body around the floor as smoothly as a professional. And in spite of herself, in spite of her own deep-seated tension, she felt herself relaxing into him.

Why fight it? It was all for appearances, after all. Soon they could go back to being enemies. Soon this momentary respite in their battle would be over. But at least for now there was a kind of truce, where time and resentment were suspended in the magic of the music and the dance. And the thought came from nowhere that if it felt this good to dance with this man when he hated you and you hated him, how much better must it feel if they actually loved each other?

She jerked her head away from his shoulder, snapping her eyes open and her thoughts back from the brink. She had no right to ask such questions. No right to wonder anything except when this interminable ordeal of being in Yannis's arms would be over. What she needed was a distraction from her thoughts, and conversation was the only tool she had to hand.

'I take it you've never married.'

She felt his intake of breath rather than heard it, felt

it in the brief falter in his step and the slight jerk of his head above hers. 'Not yet.'

'No need to sound defensive,' she responded with a nerve she didn't know she possessed. 'I'm sure there's hope for you yet.' Couples began drifting onto the dance floor around them, men and women with smiling faces in dusted-off suits and brightly coloured Sunday-best dresses. 'So why is it proving so difficult?' she persisted. 'What is it you're looking for in the woman of your dreams that's proving so elusive?'

'I don't see a ring on your finger.'

'I've been busy.'

'And I haven't?'

'*Touché*. Rafe told me you were driven to succeed. Tell me, when will you have amassed enough millions that you can settle back and relax?'

She felt his fingers tense around hers.

'I thought you had a headache.'

'It didn't get me out of dancing. Why should it preclude me from conversation?'

He spun her around a couple who cut across their path, the sudden motion leaving her momentarily breathless and giddy, her fingers biting into him for support. 'Frankly, I'm surprised you haven't,' she managed once they'd settled into a steadier rhythm again and thinking that if she kept talking, he might not notice how desperately she'd just grabbed for him. 'I know people have always liked to label you and Rafe as playboys, but of the two of you, somehow I always picked you for a family man. I would have expected you to have been married long before now.'

'Maybe I should have been!' His voice was gruff as his feet ground to a sudden halt. He looked around at the couples filling the dance floor, as if assessing whether they'd done enough to satisfy their duty, before releasing her suddenly as if deciding they had. 'Now you can go.'

CHAPTER TWO

WOMEN and headaches. Women with headaches. Who needed them?

Yannis tugged at his tie, then removed his gold and onyx striped cufflinks and let them clatter to the bedside table as he kicked off his shoes, taking in the empty suite and the king-sized four-poster bed with more than a touch of regret.

He could have brought Susannah. He hadn't had to terminate their arrangement when he had, even if it had made so much sense at the time. Apart from her own tendency to play the headache card, it was always a risk, he knew, taking any woman to a wedding and expecting her to come away without thoughts of wedding gowns and honeymoons planted in her head.

But if he had brought her, at least he'd have someone here now. Someone to rub his shoulders and massage his temples and soothe this other throbbing part of him… *Kolasi.* Why the hell he felt like sex when he'd had to endure the worst night of his life was beyond him.

No, not the worst night of his life. That black night

and the explosion of events it had detonated belonged to a time thirteen years ago. Tonight might have been uncomfortable, unpleasant at times, but nothing could surpass that poisoned night.

Still, surely he deserved some kind of compensation after having to face Marietta again? He reefed off his shirt and slung it to the floor before launching himself onto the bed, gazing unseeingly at the canopy above his head.

She'd taken offence to his comment that she'd changed, but there was no denying it. She'd grown into her body in the intervening years, her breasts fuller than he remembered, with hips that balanced their weight and rendered her shape more womanly than before.

He closed his eyes, but the pictures were still vivid of Marietta lying naked in his bed, her blonde hair like a halo around her head, the dip of her slim waist and the spring of blonde curls at the apex of her thighs, and the unmistakable mark on her breast where his teeth had bruised her perfect skin…

And yet it was the look in her eyes that had burned deeper than any memory. Wounded and hurt as he'd banished her from his bed and from his life.

He punched his pillow into submission before settling back down. She'd changed all right. Not that it mattered to him one way or another how she looked.

He sighed and folded his arms behind his head, restless and dissatisfied, wanting to put all thoughts of her out of his head and failing as another snippet from tonight's encounter wormed its way into his mind. She'd said she'd thought him a family man. Maybe long ago he had been. But that was before he'd learned what families expected of their own.

And even though he'd never married Elena in the end—*not after that night*—the relief had been short-lived, the ensuing financial fallout consuming all his attention. It had taken years of working alongside Rafe to recover the family fortune, years when he'd pushed himself mentally in order to come up with the kind of deals that would garner millions, years in which he'd pushed himself physically, spending hours in the gym, honing muscles that would keep his body as exercised as his mind. And all those years there had been no time for women in his life, unless they came with a warm body, a cold heart and a definite use by date.

No, marriage and family had no place on his list of priorities.

None whatsoever.

He was already taking breakfast when she came down. Marietta hesitated before stepping out onto the vine-covered terrace, needing a moment to gather her thoughts while she took in the picture of Yannis sitting at the table with his back to her, sipping his coffee and reading the papers.

She considered turning around and withdrawing—she could always get something delivered to her room—had half convinced herself to do so, when he seemed somehow to sense her presence and look over his shoulder. Only for a second, but he'd seen her. The cold acknowledgment in his eyes had been enough to tell her that. And she knew that if she disappeared now, it would look as if she was running away. He'd already accused her once of being afraid. She would not give him the satisfaction of thinking so again.

So instead she steeled her shoulders and pushed herself from her vantage point, the kitten heels of her sandals clicking rhythmically as she crossed the tiled terrace. In a world suddenly shrunken to this one shaded terrace and the man occupying it, the noise seemed bold. Therapeutic. *Necessary.*

For why should she shrink away and make a quiet approach? She had nothing to be ashamed of. She'd made an embarrassing mistake when she was just a teenager, she'd accepted it and got on with her life. She'd dealt with it. He was clearly the one with the problem.

'*Buongiorno,*' she called, determined to be upbeat and not show him how much she wished she could avoid another encounter with him and so soon. 'What a perfect day for a wedding.'

And it was. Above them the sky was an endless blue, while the sun cast jewels upon the azure sea beneath, with only the shard of rock known as Iseo's Pyramid, the remnants of an ancient caldera, slicing through the perfect water.

She turned her back from the view and sat down opposite him, her bravado not extending to trusting herself to meet his eyes. And yet something, whether it be curiosity, mere impulse, or a compulsion she had no way of fighting, made her lift her gaze to his face.

She should have known he would be looking at her.

For a moment their eyes connected, almost fused, before she managed to tear her eyes away and instruct the maid who had just appeared to fill her coffee cup, grateful for the diversion.

'Sleep well?' she asked, some inner minx determined to provoke him, anything not to let him see how much he rattled her. She hadn't, and it had taken her some time this morning to repair the damage of a broken sleep. And if the tightness around his eyes was any indication…

He folded the newspaper he'd been reading and sat back in his chair, planting his hands behind his head. Lazy movements, every one of them, and yet every one of them compulsive viewing. 'I slept fine.'

'Excellent,' she said, smiling too enthusiastically. If she'd needed a reminder of the width of his chest or the muscled firmness of his torso, he'd just given it to her. Along with a glimpse of olive skin with just a dusting of dark hair in the vee at his open-necked shirt. 'I'm so pleased.' She pounced on the yoghurt, drizzling on some island honey and declining an offer of pastries and bread. 'I'm meeting Sienna at ten,' she offered by way of an explanation that wasn't needed other than to give her mind something neutral to focus on. 'I don't have long.'

'Wouldn't you be better having a decent breakfast?'

'There's something indecent about yoghurt and honey? I never realised.'

She lifted the spoon to her mouth, aware that he was watching her every move, and a flash of annoyance was replaced by another, more sinful, urge.

Let him watch.

She paused, her lips slightly parted, her eyes half closed in anticipation, before she fully opened her mouth and swept the thick creamy yoghurt from the spoon.

There was definitely something indecent about her mouth. As he watched, a speck of honey clung to one lip, a tiny dew drop that caught the sun and glistened gold, and he had to fight every part of himself to remain in his chair and not lean over and remove it himself. If only he could work out how to do it without her knowing. He was still watching, mesmerised, when the tip of her pink tongue emerged and licked it from lips that settled back into a smile.

She might well have licked him. Electricity sizzled its way south as he remembered a time when she had. Virgin that she was, tentative though it had been, she'd touched him with her tongue. Tasted him.

And it hadn't been enough.

'It's good,' she said, scooping her spoon into her bowl once again? 'Maybe you should indulge in something indecent yourself.'

'I've already ordered my breakfast,' he growled, looking away, her words grating on some dark, unfamiliar part of him, but more disturbingly, arousing him in a way he'd thought impossible. But also proving a point that was more than satisfying. He'd caught her out. She'd been wrong when she'd said she'd changed. She'd claimed she'd grown up and yet here she was, still playing silly sexual games. *So much for growing up.*

He pushed his chair back and strode to the edge of the terrace, wanting an end to it, needing space, both mentally and physically. On the level below an infinity pool stretched to the cliff, merging with the brilliant blue sea beyond, a sea interrupted by nothing more than the occasional vessel and the sharp black rock that lay kilometres offshore. Even from this distance it looked like a mountain, seabirds forming an ever-changing cloud at its peak. And something Raphael had mentioned cut through the resistance he felt at extending his dealings with this woman.

'Tell me, is that where Sienna's helicopter crashed?'

Marietta followed his gaze and shivered in spite of the sun, remembering the day she'd arrived here on Montvelatte and the anticipation she'd felt to be meeting Rafe's fiancée, only for her almost to be lost before they had even met. 'Iseo's Pyramid? That's right.'

'What happened? Raphael said she was lucky to be alive. I didn't press him for details.'

He didn't turn around, just continued to gaze out over the sea, and for that she was glad. The memories of that day, the fear of not knowing whether Sienna was alive or dead, and the look of anguish she'd seen in her brother's eyes when he'd thought he'd lost the woman he loved were still fresh and raw and more than enough to contend with without Yannis's piercing gaze to throw her further off balance.

So she safely addressed her comments to the back that was turned to her and to the close-fitting shirt stretched even tighter as he crossed his arms in front of him. 'There was an unseasonal summer storm that day. It had been building slowly for hours but when it hit, it was ferocious and wild. Sienna was a passenger in a helicopter when lightning struck the rock, scattering the sea birds and sending them panicked in all directions. The pilot had no way of avoiding them. The helicopter was hit, one of the birds crashing through the cockpit and knocking out the pilot.'

He turned so suddenly she jumped, feeling caught out. 'What in God's name was she doing out there in a helicopter in the midst of a storm?'

Marietta looked away, doing her best to forget about the play of fabric against firm flesh and remember back to that dark day and the anguish that had driven Sienna to flee, an anguish that Marietta had only become aware of in the following days when the two women had had a chance to talk. Of course, it sounded crazy that anyone would be up in a helicopter in weather like that, but at the time Sienna had been left with no choice, facing marriage to a man she loved and yet who refused to acknowledge his love for her. A man who had only realised the truth when she was gone.

But how could you explain love to a man like Yannis, who knew more about anger than he would ever know about love? She shrugged. 'Sienna simply had no choice. She had to go. As it was, the pilot was lucky she was there. Sienna managed to bring the aircraft under control long enough to make it to a tiny beach on the other side of the rock. It wasn't a pretty landing, apparently, but it saved both of them.'

'And Rafe was here on the island the whole time?'

She smiled thinly, remembering the tension of that time, remembering the look of terror on her brother's face when that single plume of smoke had been sighted. 'It was a tough few hours. For everyone, but especially for Rafe. He was one of the first out with the local coast-guard, and he was there when the helicopter was found, and Sienna inside it. She had cuts and bruises but she and her babies were miraculously otherwise uninjured. Sienna maintains their survival proves that the Beast of Iseo is officially dead.'

He nodded and turned his attention back out to sea. He vaguely remembered the legend of the Beast of Iseo, where once a month the beast of the rock would rise, trawling the surrounding waters, hungry for wayward travellers and those blown off course.

It was funny how some people liked to define their monsters by the calendar. He'd learned that life wasn't that simple. Life had shown him that monsters and dangers were there every day of your life. Not dictated by a calendar. More likely dictated by a woman. And in his case, the woman sitting behind him now.

Just one day, he promised himself as his fingers curled into fists, just one more day and he would be gone from here. *Gone from her.*

'You sound like you've taken the Montvelatte customs to heart,' he said, finally turning away from the rock and forcing himself back down opposite her as his breakfast was served. 'Does that mean you'll be staying here now you're a princess?'

She laughed, knowing he'd been serious when he asked the question. 'You make it sound like being a princess is a career choice.'

'You have something better to do?'

She flashed him a glare, but he was looking away, and it was wasted, just as she knew any barbed retort she threw at him would be. He obviously had his mind made up about her.

'You didn't know I was a jewellery designer?'

'That's a full-time job?'

She chose to answer a different question. 'My partner, Xavier, and I are actually just about to embark on a major expansion, with a gallery and showroom opening shortly in Honolulu, and we're both really excited about it. So thank you, but, yes, while I'm not sure if it's "better", I do have something *else* to do.'

Xavier? He ignored her correction and focused in on the surprise element in her words. He hadn't realised she was attached, especially given her comment last night about being too busy. Clearly she wasn't *that* busy. Although, was it any real surprise? Given the ease with which she'd offered herself to him, she was bound to have found herself someone else willing to accept an offer of her charms. Probably many someones.

'So where is this Xavier? Why isn't he here with you?'

It was the look on her face that told him he'd demanded rather than asked his questions.

'Because the opening is in less than two weeks. Apart from which, why should he be invited?'

'You were the one who said he was your partner.'

She blinked, slowly and purposefully, and he immediately regretted pressing the point and giving the impression that it mattered to him in the least. It didn't, of course; his interest was merely in shooting holes in her argument. There were bound to be plenty of those.

'Xavier Delahunty,' she began after a measured breath, 'is my *business* partner, and together we own Paua International, a small but growing jewellery concern. Xavier handles the business side of things while I'm the head designer. We've been working with paua and silver designs in Auckland for a few years but slowly incorporating pacific pearls into the equation.

'When the new gallery opens in Honolulu,' she continued, 'we'll launch the new collection with it. If it goes well, we have plans to expand further into the US and Europe.'

Not many things took Yannis Markides by surprise. Not many people. But not for the first time, this woman did.

'I didn't realise you had a job.'

'No? I suppose you imagined I've just been swanning around, princess-in-waiting these last few years. Whereas you've been amassing so much money you haven't had time to breathe. Why are you so driven, Yannis? Is money so sexy that you'd rather have a fortune than a wife?'

Any hint of remorse that he might have misjudged her was consumed in the heat that speared up inside him, a tidal wave of resentment that brought with it more than a hint of satisfaction. This was more like it, more of what he expected from someone like her.

No surprises there at all.

'Maybe,' he replied, 'it would have been nice to have had the choice.'

She looked up him, cat-like eyes narrowed and searching for the meaning behind his cryptic comment, the question already forming on those sultry lips. A question that never came as the maid interrupted with more coffee, and he turned back to his meal, suddenly reminded of his hunger and the reason he was out here on this terrace. Not to settle old scores, nor even to relive the circumstances that had given birth to them, but simply to break his fast. To slake his early morning thirst and hunger.

And that hunger had nothing to do with her!

Sienna was still enjoying a scented bubble bath when Marietta arrived at her suite. Her dresser, Carmelina, was fussing over her, bringing towels and catering to her every need, and Marietta was grateful to have a few moments to collect her thoughts. Meeting with Yannis on the terrace had rattled her, and much more than she'd realised at the time, leaving her feeling shaky, her emotions shredded. For Yannnis appeared determined to dislike her, even to hate her no matter what she did or said, and still she had no real inkling why. But whatever it was she was supposed to have done in the past, he certainly seemed to bring out the worst in her now.

She wasn't a bad person, she was sure of it. She wasn't perfect either, far from it, but why Yannis held her in such contempt was beyond her. She'd gone to his bed. Offered herself to him. Made a stupid fool of herself in the process. But beyond that, what had she done that was so unforgivable?

Forget him! Tomorrow would bring escape and escape couldn't come soon enough. Tomorrow she would go to Hawaii and focus on the launch and the new gallery and getting back to her career and her life, and bury all thoughts of Yannis Markides in the process. His place was in the past. And in the past was where he would stay.

Sienna emerged from the bathroom, wearing a veil of steam and a smile so wide and joyous it rendered Yannis's puzzling behaviour irrelevant. 'I'm marrying Rafe today,' she told Marietta, as if she had said, 'I can't believe it's really happening.' The love beamed out of her soon-to-be sister-in-law's face as Marietta wrapped her in her arms and gave her a hug. And once again, the sheer wonder of witnessing a love so true—a love that was returned—blew her away. Marietta smiled and breathed in the good vibes, knowing without a doubt that her brother was one lucky man.

Organ music filled the ancient church, sending already high spirits soaring with the lofty notes. Cameras were discreetly placed, covering all the angles, ready to transmit pictures of the world's latest royal wedding around the globe.

By normal standards, the wedding was small. By royal standards, minute, with just a single attendant for the bride and groom, but recent events in the tiny principality ensured the world's attention. After the fall from grace of its former Prince and his family, everyone wanted to witness the fairy-tale wedding between the bastard Prince and his helicopter pilot bride, the media openly wondering if such a match could work.

Standing by his side, feeling Rafe's nerves and at the same time his anticipation, Yannis was in no doubt that Rafe would make it work. His best friend stood waiting for his bride to appear, his hands clasped firmly behind his back, a fine sheen of moisture just visible on his brow as he smiled and made small talk and kept looking over his shoulder, probably without even realising he was doing so. It was the first time in his life Yannis had ever seen Rafe looking anything approximating nervous, and it was unnerving.

Would he feel the same way if he ever married? Would he feel that nervous tug of emotion that seemed to hold his best friend in its thrall? He doubted it. The closest brush he'd had with marriage had been part of a business deal with no emotions involved, if you didn't count the lingering resentment that a marriage had even been required. But while that marriage hadn't eventuated, he could appreciate now that a marriage based around sound business principles did make a lot of sense. That would be what he'd choose for himself now. If he'd been interested, that was. Something simple, mutually beneficial, economically sound.

Unemotional.

The music changed suddenly then, the organist signalling the arrival of the bride. 'Beautiful,' he heard the groom say, and he turned, and a boulder he didn't even realise was sitting in his gut dropped a level.

'She is,' he heard himself say, knowing, even as he

uttered the words, that they were talking about different women. He had no problem with that. One glance had told him that Sienna looked stunning, her red-lit hair coiled high on her head, a gauzy tiara-anchored veil doing nothing to hide the smile that illuminated her face as she walked towards the man she was about to marry.

But it was the vision of Marietta that pulled his gaze and held it hostage, Marietta, who preceded the bride up the aisle, her dress an echo of the bride's fitted sheath but in a rich golden fabric that reflected the colours of the stained glass windows back at him with every movement, transforming her into a work of art.

Work of art nothing. She was a goddess. When had the teenager become a siren? *A temptress.* Because hadn't she tempted him today with her mouth, goading him with her words, teasing him with her pink tongue?

And now she walked towards him, her lips slick with colour and her eyes rimmed with kohl, with a body that was made for sex. Sex he'd once been offered on a plate. Sex he'd turned down.

Logic deserted him in those moments as she took her final few steps toward the altar. Why had he turned her away? What madness had he been suffering? For a man would have to be mad to turn such a woman away.

Marietta drew close, her eyes sliding every which way but in his direction, and it was sheer force of will that pulled them to his and held them there. He felt the quiver in their blue depths and could almost read the questions there; he felt the tremor that skittered down her spine in a heated echo in his own until she broke contact on a swallow, forcing her head to turn away. She sent a benevolent smile to Rafe, despite the fact her brother was still totally engrossed in the woman behind her, and a stab of something like jealousy speared him deep inside. A reaction that made no sense. Rafe was her family, her very own brother. Why shouldn't she smile at him like that, and why did he care if she did? And yet it still rankled as she took her place on the opposite side, making way for Sienna, and Yannis took advantage of the moment to breathe some sense into himself.

She shouldn't have this effect on him. She couldn't. And yet his palms were clammy, his pulse erratic, and none of it made sense. But as Sienna joined Rafe at the altar, the pair exchanging a quiet word before she took his arm and they faced the front, there was one thing he knew beyond doubt. He wanted that smile for himself. *He wanted her.*

Thirteen years ago he'd had a glimpse of paradise, a glimpse that had been savagely denied him by circumstances, even if the decision had been his own. And yet he'd paid the price then as surely as if he had taken her, and he'd been paying the price every day of his life since. An endless slog of trying to win back what had been lost. What he had lost because she had turned up in his bed.

Tonight was his chance to take what he was owed. Tonight was his chance to get even.

And *sto thiavolo*, he damn well would!

CHAPTER THREE

THE wedding was long, the reception a banquet ten times bigger and more sumptuous than last night's lavish, yet still simpler affair, and no matter where she was in the large room, no matter where she turned in an attempt to escape, it was always Yannis who filled her line of sight, Yannis who occupied centre stage.

And it had been that way ever since she'd walked down that aisle. She'd tried to look anywhere but at him, battled to keep her eyes on Rafe, or on the assembled crowd of dignitaries and guests, but a force she had no way of fighting had compelled her to look his way, and what she'd seen in his eyes had shaken her to the very core.

He was still angry. It was there in his bearing, in the tension that lined his shoulders. But now there was a new energy in his eyes, a hunger that frightened her with its intensity. A hunger that was directed at her.

She turned away from another sudden encounter, another uncomfortable and sizzling meeting of eyes, and headed towards the refreshment table. Only a few hours to go, she told herself as she picked up a glass of sparkling lemon water, relishing the burst of coolness against her hand and down her throat like a lifeline. Every part of her felt overheated. Every part of her felt hot. But just a few short hours more and the wedding would be over, and she could leave Montvelatte.

She'd miss her brother and his new wife, who had made the move beyond sister-in-law to friend even before today's wedding ceremony, but at least she'd had some time with them before the wedding, time thankfully spent without Yannis's blatant disapproval. And, anyway, in a few months, when Sienna's twins were born, she could return. Meanwhile she would leave the island knowing without a shadow of a doubt, that her brother and his wife were soulmates.

She put down her glass, glancing up as an ancient clock rang out the hour. Damn. It was time. She dragged in a breath tinged with a heady dose of frustration. She wasn't ready to dance with him again, not after last night, but especially not after the look she'd seen in his eyes when she'd walked down that aisle.

Not when it had made her feel things she had no wish to feel.

How could he do this to her, turn her emotions around with just one heated look, one searing gaze? Because somehow he'd gone from being a man who hated her—a simple emotion she could understand, if not the reason why—to a man who sent messages with his eyes that took her thoughts and emotions in a different direction entirely.

Damn him! Why must he plague her with this emotional roller coaster? Because that was exactly how it felt. It had been easier before, when her words had rankled him, digging under his skin and turning his resentment into something three-dimensional, something real. But now the dynamic seemed to have changed. Now she didn't know what he wanted, the messages he was sending just as real, yet illogical, and it bothered her.

She sidestepped a group, exchanging pleasantries as she skirted the crowd, anxious to find Sienna to see if she needed any help with her dress or make-up before the obligatory dance and the photographers that would accompany it.

But it was Yannis who emerged in front of her. 'I've been looking for you.'

She stopped, her heart tripping in her chest. She didn't need or want to know why. Just the knowledge that he was looking for her was too much, too intrusive. She put a hand to her chest, wanting to ensure her heart stayed there, on the inside. 'Excuse me. I have to see if Sienna needs anything.' She made a move to go past him, but he held her in check with one hand on her arm. Gentle but firm.

'Sienna is fine.'

She looked down at his hand, her gaze tracing the line of his arm, and she tugged against his grip. He didn't let go. 'What do you think you're doing?'

'I have a proposition for you.'

She looked up at him, baffled by the urgency that accompanied his words, knowing it could bode no good. 'I'm not interested.'

From somewhere behind him the strains of the orchestra started up, applause breaking out as Rafe escorted his new bride onto the dance floor, and Marietta cursed that she'd been so intent on avoiding Yannis that she'd abandoned her duties altogether. She felt him press her arm again, more insistently this time.

'You haven't heard me out yet.'

'So tell me what it is. And then I'll say no.'

He smiled, his teeth dazzlingly cool and white in his olive-skinned face, while something in his dark eyes glowed hot. 'First, we dance.'

In a way, it should have been easier. They'd done this last night, been in each other's arms, pretending to be a couple. They'd battled through their first awkward steps until they'd achieved some kind of rhythm.

And yet it wasn't easy. From the moment Yannis took her in his arms, she felt that something had changed. The fury had peeled away, and there was a smouldering, simmering tension underlying every movement, every look, and no longer was she merely dealing with a man who hated her. Now she was dealing with a man who wanted something from her, who wanted to make her a proposition.

And this man was an entirely more dangerous beast.

She steeled herself against his touch, telling herself he didn't affect her, but it was no use. She could feel his want in every brush of cloth against cloth. She could read his need in every place his body pressed against her. And she knew without a doubt that he could read hers.

He said nothing as they danced. Nothing as he spun

her around, their bodies working together with ridiculous ease given their first clumsy pairing. And yet he said so much with just a glance, a velvet look, and with the hungry splay of his fingers on the skin of her back.

None of her senses were safe. He assailed her on every level and then some. She couldn't look at him without being challenged by that dark gaze, couldn't breathe without drawing his signature scent into her very being, that same scent distilling into taste on her tongue. His touch was everywhere around her, his heartbeat in her ear, solid and strong.

And as for rational thought? That had long since fled. Fully clothed, in a room full of people, and all she could think about was this man. This man, and how he made her feel. He banished every other thought from her head.

It made no sense. Didn't he hate her? And yet right at this moment he made her feel that she mattered, and that she was at the very epicentre of his existence. And after thirteen years of knowing how much he resented her, after witnessing the evidence of that with her own eyes when they'd been reintroduced just last night, and felt again at breakfast when his eyes had bored into her, cold and sharp, this sudden turnaround was unfathomable. Unbelievable.

Which didn't explain why a part of her—a part she'd long thought bitterly twisted and rent from her that savage night so long ago, but, strangely, still there—wanted to cling on to the fantasy.

She'd given up fantasising about him long ago. She'd moved on, in her career and in her life. And yet now she felt as if the years had fallen away and she was back, a teenager with a crush, an itch, an obsession that refused to go away.

And then they stopped moving, and she blinked back into reality, her senses widening their focus. At some time the dance floor had filled, and they were surrounded by elegantly attired couples waiting for the next dance to begin. There was conversation and laughter and the glint of a thousand carats or more sprayed artistically across every wrist and neck and head, and she'd not noticed a thing.

She stepped back, aware she had made no attempt to move from his hold, suddenly afraid. How much did this man affect her that she would notice nothing of what was going on around her? And worse, after what he'd done to her once before, how could she let him?

Panic hit her hard, shredding to tatters what was left of the all-encompassing spell he'd woven around her. She didn't know the answer to her questions. All she knew was that she had to get away. Had to protect herself.

She spun away, lurching from the dance floor, making for the closest French windows that she knew would lead to the outside, where there would be space and freedom and air in abundance, surely enough to clear the dizziness affecting her.

'Where are you going?'

'I need some air.'

The fairy-lit terrace was a world between two worlds, on one side the glittering ballroom with its crystal chandeliers and golden light and an ever-changing kaleidoscope of colour as guests whirled around the dance floor, and on the other, moonlight dancing on the water, stars winking above, sequins twinkling in the velvet perfection of the night.

It was quieter here and cooler, but the night air was more then welcome after the fire he had brought to her belly.

'Can I get you anything?'

Of course he had followed her. He had a proposition to put to her, and she'd fled before he'd had the chance. But she didn't turn, didn't want or need to look at him, not when she needed to be able to think. And not when she feared he might take her back to that place where the world fell away and nothing else mattered. She didn't like how it felt. Didn't know what it meant. And, damn him, she wasn't going back to that place again.

'I'm fine,' she lied.

'Are you? Only you looked—'

'Tired?' she interjected, moving further along the terrace, knowing full well he hadn't been about to say anything of the sort. 'Well, it's been a long day.'

'No, not tired,' he said, remaining at her shoulder, 'I was going to say you looked shocked. Even a bit stunned.'

She gave what she hoped would pass for a laugh. 'Did I? Is it any wonder. I guess it was surprising that we made it through an entire dance this time without arguing.'

'I don't think that's the reason.'

'Should I care what you think?'

A breeze caught her gown, rippling the fabric around her legs and bringing with it the scent of jasmine and rosemary and a hundred other scents of the island. *And the man at her shoulder.*

She shivered, but from the inside out. Hadn't he invaded her senses enough? Now she didn't even have to look at him to feel his imprint on her very soul. She didn't want it there, didn't want these heightened senses plaguing her. She wanted to be gone from here, back at work. She wanted to be herself again.

Tomorrow couldn't come soon enough.

There was no point staying outside; her sanctuary had been shot to hell. She turned, circling him so she wouldn't have to look at him. 'I should go back inside.'

His hand caught hers, arresting her escape.

'Sienna—' she protested.

'Is fine without you. She has Raphael to take care of her.'

'But still…'

'We haven't spoken yet about my proposition.' Still she didn't look at him, just felt the pressure of his hand around hers, the gentle stroke of his thumb against the back of her hand.

'I already told you, the answer is no.'

'You haven't even heard what it is.'

His thumb kept up its gentle massage, each stroke like a call to her body, an invitation. A promise.

She swallowed, looking at the open doors to the ballroom as if they were a lifeline, saw the guests milling inside, heard the tinkle of laughter and crystal, and knew that was her world. Knew that was where she belonged. But right now she had no clue how to get back.

'Look at me,' he said, guiding her chin with his free hand until she faced him. 'Look at me,' he repeated when she kept her eyes downcast.

Slowly, reluctantly, she raised them until they jagged on his. A smile teased the corners of his lips, and suddenly he looked years younger, like the Yannis of her youth. 'That's better.' And even the tone of his voice fed into her soul. His hand circled her neck, his fingers stroking into the hair at her nape, and she shuddered into his touch.

'You're so beautiful,' he said.

And a snatch of memory played vividly through her mind, of the three of them, her, Rafe and Yannis, on the last day of their summer holiday together in the south of France, the summer she'd turned sixteen. They'd ridden horses along the beach and had a picnic lunch in the middle of a field of wild poppies, and she and Yannis had collapsed on the ground to stare at the sky while Rafe returned the horses. And Yannis had reached over while she was lying on her back and placed a flower behind her ear. 'You're beautiful,' he'd said, his hand sliding through her hair as he'd dipped his head and kissed her.

And something squeezed tight in her chest at the memory, something she didn't quite understand and didn't want to analyse too closely. Because Yannis meant nothing to her. Nothing but the memory of teenaged dreams crushed so violently and vehemently she would never make that mistake again.

She reared back. 'You can't do this.'

'I can't do what?' he asked, refusing to let her go.

'This?' And he took her hand to his mouth and turned it and opened her palm to his mouth. Hot. Wet. His lips and breath engaged in a dance of sensuality, his tongue turning the dance erotic. She shuddered, gasping as the lave of his tongue reached places it had no way of reaching. She felt his answering smile on her palm, witnessed it as he slowly pulled away.

'Or this?'

He was going to kiss her. He gave her plenty of warning, surely enough time to escape or at least turn her head away. Or was there no time? Had time stood still on this fairy-lit terrace suspended against the inky sea and sky?

No time, she decided as his lips met hers. No time to think, or protest or flee. No time to object to the press of his mouth on hers, the coaxing of his lips, the lure of his open-mouthed heat.

No time but now.

Liquid heat infused her veins, and as his mouth and lips and tongue meshed with hers, fire swallowed her whole. Sensation upon sensation, his kiss deepened, building, his hands at her back, behind her head she could feel him everywhere, and it was too much for her senses to deal with, and yet still it wasn't enough, and she wanted more.

She'd been expecting a kiss. Anticipating it. But she'd never expected this. And through the sensual tide washing over her, it occurred to her that someone had made a huge error. That something that engendered feelings so enormous and amazing could be summed up in one insignificant word was wrong.

This was not just a kiss, it was richer, deeper, with texture and rhythm and life. And she wanted more.

His breathing as ragged as her own, he took her face in his hands and drew away. 'Make love with me tonight.'

And more took on a whole new meaning. Her heart was thumping, her breathing choppy, her lips felt plumped and tender. 'It's crazy,' she said, because she couldn't say no, even though she knew she should. Even though she was crazy to even consider saying yes.

'You want me,' he countered. 'And I've wanted you ever since I saw you last night. Ever since I took you in my arms.'

She shook her head, the pain of that night thirteen years ago refusing to be ignored. 'You had your chance. You threw me out.'

'A long time ago.'

'You hate me.'

'I want you.'

'And I hate you!'

'Do you? You didn't kiss me like you hated me.'

'This makes no sense.'

'Who needs to analyse it? All I know is that I want you. Tonight.' He pressed his lips to hers once again, let them linger, a powerful reminder of what he could do, an echo of how he could make her feel with just one touch. 'We both leave tomorrow. We can both leave angry, or we can leave satisfied. Your choice.'

Her teeth found one kiss-swollen lip, and she raked them over its unfamiliar plumpness. 'One night.'

'Just one night. And then we go our separate ways.'

'And this is your proposition.'

'Do you have a better one?'

His fingers were doing something behind her ears, tracing lazy circles that sent sensations curling down like ribbons inside her, caressing her doubts, smoothing her fears with a cool satin edge.

'But the reception—'

'After the reception,' he said, brushing aside her pathetic attempt at delay as easily as he brushed a stray tendril of hair from her brow. 'I will come to your room. Just one night. Do we have a deal?'

How many nights had she lain awake and wondered? How many times had she imagined what it would have been like to make love to him, if only he hadn't discovered her identity? How would it feel to have him inside her? She remembered the feel of him nudging at her—the pressure—and the insane and unstoppable compulsion that had come from somewhere to have him fill her. Complete her. But it had never happened, and she'd been thrown from his room, feeling gutted. Empty. Bereft.

And now he was offering her one night. One night to find out the answers to so many questions. Would she be mad to take it? Or madder to refuse? If she turned him down she might hold the moral high ground, but she would never know.

Was it worth it?

Her body hummed with expectation, secret places in her body pulsed with new life. Secret places that would soon be secret no longer. And yes, the compulsion was still there, the need to take him inside her, newly awakened and hungering for the feast.

He wanted her. She could have him. What was to decide?

'Yes,' she whispered on the softly scented night breeze.

'What was that?'

'Yes,' she heard herself say again, her voice coming from a very long way away. 'You've got a deal.'

He pulled her into his arms then, full length against his body so she could be in no mistake about his urgent need, his mouth crashing down on hers, a hard kiss, a hungry kiss, all too brief but no less powerful for its brevity, leaving her reeling in its wake.

'Tonight,' he said, as he led her back towards the reception. 'Wait for me.'

CHAPTER FOUR

IT WAS impossible to focus after that. The wedding passed in a blur of conversation and protocol, too quickly for Marietta's liking and yet at the same time much too slowly. For through it all, there was Yannis, biding his time and watching her. Waiting. The glint in his eyes spoke to her of his desire, the touch of his hand at her elbow or the merest brush of his hand against hers setting her body alight and promising so much more.

In every possible way he was letting her know, reminding her that he was waiting for this wedding to be over and for the chance for them to be alone. And even the fear she felt that, in the insanity of agreeing to sleep with a man who seemed to hate her, she was making the biggest mistake of her life was not enough to counter the sense of anticipation coiling like a hungry beast inside her.

Finally the long wedding and reception were over, the bride and groom cheered on their way, the guests filtering away until she fled herself, feeling giddy and sick as the beast twisted and thrashed inside her, refusing to let her body escape the turmoil of her mind. Alone in her room, she paced the floor. She should have been exhausted, but a day filled with a broiling sexual tension had seen her senses primed. Anticipation kept them there.

Anticipation and a growing nervousness. It could be hours before the Castello settled down, hours she had to fill, and what had seemed so obvious out there on the fairy-lit terrace, so logical, now seemed to defy everything she had ever held dear.

One night with Yannis! She might as well spend it with the devil. Hadn't she just spent the last thirteen years telling herself she was over him? Trying to obliterate every last memory of the man? And now she was expecting him to come knocking at her door. What had she been thinking?

She'd been thinking that she wanted him and that now was her chance. Her one and only chance.

And if it ended badly too? She was no fragile teenager any more, but how long would it take her to get over it this time? Why was she even giving him a second chance?

Frustrated with the mess that was her head, she headed for the bathroom, determined to do something other than wear a track in the carpet. But pulling off the golden gown and stepping out of her underwear merely raised a whole new set of questions that proved once again how logic had eluded her when she'd made this crazy deal. Once she'd showered, what was she supposed to wear?

More to the point, what would he be expecting? Certainly not the comfortable cotton shorts and singlet top she usually wore to bed.

Cursing herself for her own naivety, she let the torrent from the shower massage shoulders tense from too many questions and not enough answers. What was to say he'd even turn up? He'd come up with this crazy plan in a heartbeat. What was to say he wouldn't change his mind just as quickly?

Then she remembered the heated promise in his eyes as they'd left the ballroom, and the feel of his thumb tracing a path down her arm as they'd parted, and she knew he would not change his mind. *He would come.*

The contents of the suite's spacious wardrobes offered her some hope. She finally settled on a cream-coloured silken nightgown, modest in design without being prudish, that slipped over her skin like a kiss. She shivered, her skin tingling with the knowledge of the kisses to come, firming her breasts and hardening her nipples, and she knew there was no way she could let him see her like this, so she pulled a voluminous robe from the wardrobe and wrapped it around her, pulling the tie tight, reasserting control with it. Instantly she felt better. She was no seductress. A lamb being led to the slaughter was more like it, a slaughter she'd practically invited upon herself.

She collapsed into a chair, pulled the pins from her hair and attacked its length with a brush, stroke after stroke after stroke. Her scalp tingled, protesting against the abuse, her brushstrokes turning her hair into a blonde veil with the static electricity. *Stroke. Stroke. Stroke.* So frantic that when the knock came, she barely heard it over the swish of the brush through her hair. He was already inside by the time she'd turned, delight that he had come and fear of what would happen next combining with the surge of adrenaline.

He'd removed his tie, undone the buttons at his throat, but the look was nowhere near casual, not with the set of his jaw and the gleam in his eyes.

So tall. So intent. *So dangerous.*

His lips curved into a crooked smile while his gaze drank her in. 'You didn't lock the door.'

'You thought I'd change my mind?'

He paused before answering, his eyes so hungry they seemed ready to devour her whole and yet so filled with turmoil that she knew he was driven by his own beast that matched her own. 'Not a chance.'

She stood and turned to face him then, on legs suddenly rubbery and weak, wishing strength into her bones and courage into her spirit. How could he be so sure of her when she was so unsure of herself?

Her brush felt heavy in one hand. Solid. Real. Her other hand plucked nervously at the tie at her waist, and she wished she'd thought to dim the lights, if only so it might disguise her burning cheeks. But if she looked skittish, she didn't have to act it. He wasn't the only one who could sound so businesslike.

'Well, then. Seeing you're here, I guess we might as well get on with it.'

He crossed the floor as soundlessly as a big cat, his

long-limbed strides eating up the distance between them, all predatory power and gleaming intent. 'What's the hurry, Princess? We've got all night.' He took the brush from her hand, dropping it to the floor and curling his fingers into her hair. 'You looked beautiful tonight with your hair up, but this is better. Much better.' He kissed the top of her head, his fists making bunches in her hair behind her head that he tugged down so she had no choice but to raise her face to his.

She shuddered under his touch, melting into it despite her jangling nerves and thumping heart.

'*Ise thea,*' he said in Greek. 'You are a goddess.' His lips descended on hers, and she sighed into the kiss, giving herself up to it, finding herself back in that place where the world slipped away and there was nothing but him. His hands relaxed their grip, loosening in her hair and sweeping down her back, making her more aware than she'd ever been of the contours of her own body. She felt a tug at her waist—her tie coming undone—felt the sudden sweep of air when he let the robe fall open.

Then his hands were underneath, sliding up her shoulders and shrugging off the robe, until she stood before him with just a film of silk to protect her.

'*Dios,*' he growled, and he turned her towards a mirror. 'Do you have any idea how you look? Do you have any idea how you make me feel?'

She gasped as she caught sight of herself, the silk of the gown she'd thought modest almost transparent against her skin, hiding nothing of her body from his sight. She looked at his face in the mirror, his gaze hot and heavy, and she trembled at the intensity of it.

'You can't be cold,' he murmured. And she had to agree with him, even though she shook like a new born lamb suddenly exposed to the elements. She wasn't cold. She was on fire, his kisses, his touch, even his very presence combining together to set her senses aflame and her skin alight.

Those hands now slipped over the fabric of her gown, the gossamer-thin fabric no barrier to the heated desire that came with his touch. His hands drank her in, and it was all she could do to remember to breathe. They slid down her sides, fingers moulding to her body, they slid upwards over her ribcage and scooped inwards, catching her breasts. Her breath caught, her brain function shorting as he cupped their weight, his thumbs stroking the tips of her aching nipples before he spun her easily around to face him.

She gasped into his mouth, arching her back towards him, and was immediately rewarded as he scooped her up into his arms and spun her around. She was already dizzy, her blood fizzing, her earlier nervousness that he might not turn up forgotten, her earlier fear that he might not want her put to rest.

It was Yannis who lowered her down on the wide bed. Yannis who tenderly smoothed the hair from her brow before he rose from the bed to kick off his shoes and unbutton his shirt.

Her Yannis.

And then he reefed off his shirt, and it was all she could do not to whimper. His trousers followed, unzipped and shrugged off, and she fought the urge to squirm into the coverlet.

Oh, my. She'd seen him naked before, she'd seen him aroused, but that had been thirteen long years ago. Now, even with his underwear still on, it was clear that time had just improved him.

Broad shoulders framed a chest an Olympic swimmer would be proud of, firm, wide and taut, dark-hair-dusted olive skin sweeping down to a tight packed waist and an arrow of hair that led enticingly lower to where a band of black stretched tight across his loins.

And desire competed with a rush of panic. If his blood had headed south, as that bulge attested, hers was heading north into her cheeks. Her skin flamed, her mind reeling with the impossibility of the task that lay ahead. What had she been thinking? Just like last time, there was no way she was going to be able to accommodate him, no way he wouldn't be able to tell…

He chose that moment to peel away that last remaining scrap of material, and Marietta's breath caught in her throat. What had seemed so simple hours earlier, so doable within the context of a kiss that had guaranteed everything, now felt like mission impossible.

She should say something. Wanted to say something. But her tongue was stuck to the roof of her mouth, and no words were possible. Especially not when he lowered himself alongside her, his mouth zeroing in again on hers.

And once again the word kiss didn't do it justice.

Neither the word magic. Not the way his lips moved over hers, coaxing, seducing.

Persuading.

Maybe it would work. Maybe, if he kept kissing her like this, she wouldn't feel a thing, and he would never know.

His hand found her breast, skin, silk and heat working together in perfect sensual harmony. She arched her back into his palm, wanting more. He filled his mouth with her breast, rolling his tongue around the tight bud of her nipple and sending spears of sensation to her very core, and still she wanted more. He gave her more, with his mouth, with his tongue, with his heated breath and the shift of wet silk on screaming nerve endings until even the mantra of *more* wasn't enough. She wanted it all.

Then his hands were at her thighs, smoothing silk on skin, his sensual movements moving him inexorably closer to his ultimate goal, and she became afraid again.

He was so expert.

A brush of his hands up her legs, and silk pooled at her thighs.

So practised.

His hand curved over her mound, and she gasped, his fingers perilously close to her screamingly tight bud of nerves, his erection heavy and alive against her leg.

She was a rank amateur.

His fingers dipped lower still, her internal muscles clenching involuntarily, instinctively. He growled into her mouth, and she knew he was feeling her dampness through her thin panties.

A virgin!

He released her mouth long enough for her to ask the question, 'How many women have you had?'

He stilled for just one moment. What kind of question is that?'

Her breathing was fast, it was an effort to talk, but she had to know how wide the disparity was between them. 'You have a reputation as a playboy.'

His fingers slid under the lace edge of her panties. 'I like sex. Who doesn't?'

She squirmed underneath him, shifting away, wishing she had an answer to his question. 'But how many? Ten? Twenty? Do you even know?'

His hand paused its exploration, and he looked up at her. 'Greek-Cypriot men have a reputation as excellent lovers. It's a reputation we take seriously. I promise you, you won't be disappointed.'

She might not be disappointed—how could she be when she had nothing to measure it by? But what about him? Would he laugh at her when he discovered the truth? He, who had had plenty of lovers in the intervening years, and her, with the pathetic record of not even one.

His argument made, he swept the hem of her gown higher, baring her belly, and traced her navel with his tongue before filling it with its wet heat, time after time, a precursor for the act to come. Her hands tangled in his hair. Her thoughts tangled in her head.

Oh, God, why had she ever thought this would work?

His hands caressed her waist, spanning it wide-fingered and trailing down, finding the lace of her panties and tugging down that final barrier until even that last vestige of protection was gone. She wanted to pull down her gown. She wanted to hide herself away under the covers, but she knew that if she did, he would know the truth, so she lay there, exposed to his gaze, afraid of the desire so blatant in his eyes, afraid of the power of his erection so heavy and proud between his legs. Wanting him, but so afraid.

'Beautiful,' he uttered, his hands cupping her feet as he knelt before her. Those hands moved higher as he insinuated himself between her legs, his fingertips scorching a path, trailing fire up her ankles, her shins, her knees, the liquid sensations taking the edge off her fear once more.

She could do this. Women did, all the time. It didn't have to be that hard.

'So beautiful,' he said, his hands at her thighs, his thumbs circling rhythmically 'And it will be better this time.'

She stilled under his touch. 'What do you mean, *better*?'

He dropped himself down, his hands either side of her, his mouth nuzzling at her neck.

'Simply that we are both older, more experienced. It will be better for both of us. Easier.'

Under his mouth her shoulder squirmed, protesting. It wouldn't be easier. Not for her. He was expecting her to have had other lovers to make his job easier. But had it been so difficult that night? Is that why he'd thrown her out? Because she'd been a virgin? 'What was so hard about it last time?'

He lifted his head, cursing whatever impulse had

made him bring up that other, fateful night. What did she expect him to say? That he hadn't been in a position to sleep with her, even if he'd wanted to? That he'd been committed to another woman to seal a business deal?

Why should she believe it? The marriage had never happened.

He framed his lips around one nipple, teasing it with his tongue before letting go. 'Forget I said anything.'

But she was already scrabbling up the bed, pushing herself up into the pillows and away from him.

'No. I want to know what made it so hard. Tell me, why did you throw me out of your room that night? Why is it suddenly okay to sleep with me now, and not then?'

He sat back on his knees, raking one hand through his hair, his sex-drugged brain not functioning. She took immediate advantage, rolling herself away, tugging down her gown as she circled the bed, pouncing on her robe and dragging it around her like a drowning woman reaching for a lifeline.

'What do you think?' he argued, one hand held out in front of him in supplication, 'You were my best friend's little sister.'

'And still am!'

'You were only sixteen.'

'I was old enough to know what I wanted.'

'You were a virgin!'

It was the answer she'd least wanted to hear, the answer that told her how crazy she was to have allowed herself to be in this situation now. 'And that was why you threw me out? Because I was a virgin?'

'Marietta—'

'But it's okay to sleep with me now.'

'Marietta, what is this? You're not making any sense.'

'Maybe not, but I'm seeing sense. Finally. I don't know why I thought you'd changed. But you haven't, have you? It's all about you and what you want.'

His face darkened, dark eyes narrowing as she paced around the bed, arms crossed in front of her like a shield. He propped himself up on one arm, gesturing with the other down his still naked body, his erection holding, but barely. He wanted her to look at him, wanted to see that widening of her eyes and the rush of hunger that accompanied it. 'You wanted this too! You couldn't wait to spread your legs for me tonight. I could smell it on you.'

She kept her eyes firmly fixed on his face, sending him a look that carried a thousand poisoned barbs. 'You had your chance thirteen years ago, and you blew it. Big time.'

He was rapidly losing patience, along with his erection. 'What are you playing at? You agreed to this tonight. We had a deal.'

'I changed my mind! I'd sooner make a deal with the devil. And so what if it means that you go home angry tomorrow? From what I can see, you've been angry for most of your life. Why should it matter to me?'

Sto thiavolo! There was no reasoning with the woman. What demons had possessed him to imagine that burying himself in a woman like her would ever result in anything but disaster? He was better off out of it. 'I've had enough of this!' He flung himself from the bed, sweeping up his clothes and flinging them on, all the while his eyes burning into hers as the only logical reason for her behaviour hammered home to him. 'You planned this all along, didn't you?' He picked up his shirt from the creased pile on the floor, punching one arm into a sleeve. 'Planned to get back at me for something that happened years ago when you were barely out of nappies.'

'I don't remember asking you to go to bed with me tonight.'

'I don't remember you saying no. You saw it as your pathetic little chance at revenge, and you grabbed it with both hands. And that's why you asked all those questions—how many lovers I'd had—all the time you were looking for an angle, a chance to make your move and justify your little rant.'

'You're crazy.'

'Am I? But you were so good, weren't you. You waited right to the end. It wasn't enough to stick the blade in, you had to twist it as well.'

There was a hint of a tremble about her jawline, a pink stain to her cheeks. Then she tossed her head back and swallowed. 'If that's what you want to believe, you go right ahead.'

He plunged feet into shoes that were still warm and faced her, his lip curling in disdain as he looked down upon her dishevelled hair and swollen lips, and sent up a quick prayer of thanks for whatever shred of sense had brought him back from the brink of madness. 'You said it was me who hadn't changed, but the truth is it's you who are still the same. You who are still playing adolescent games.'

'I told you, you can choose to believe what you want to.'

'Oh, don't worry about that. I will.'

Slamming a door had never felt so therapeutic. But it was nowhere near enough. He stormed back towards his suite, the ancient Castello creaking around him in the night, tapestries shifting against the walls, drapes fluttering in the turbulence as he passed.

She was a tease. Nothing but a tease. All day she'd been goading him with her words and her actions.

This was the woman whose very mouth and tongue had teased him to the brink of existence for the sake of one droplet of honey. This was the woman who'd asked him this morning if he'd like to enjoy something indecent. And he'd played into her hands like an amateur.

He couldn't wait to get off this island and get right away from her. Tomorrow couldn't come soon enough.

CHAPTER FIVE

SHE was packed and ready before six, although the helicopter taking her to Rome to connect with her flight to Honolulu wasn't due for hours. She took breakfast in her room, determined not to run across Yannis before she left, and stared moodily out of her window, watching the sea birds wheel and circle over the cliffs, wishing she could so easily fly away.

It already had the makings of another beautiful day. It would be hot later on when the sun made its presence felt, but for now the morning was crisp and clear with just a hint of a breeze, and the outside beckoned. She would be a long time on her flight, changing at Kuala Lumpur before the haul to Honolulu. She'd be wise to take the opportunity to stretch her legs while she could.

Sienna had shown her the cliff walk, and she headed for it now, circling the glistening pool before joining the path where it weaved through the low bushes, herbs and tiny flowers eking out an existence along the rock-strewn cliff-top. She walked to the look-out over the valley and the winding road that led to Velatte City and the bustling port far below. She watched the ferries steaming into port and out again, and she breathed the sweet perfumed air.

And then she turned back towards the Castello. She'd done the right thing. Hours spent tossing and turning in the darkness had convinced her of that. She couldn't have let him stay, couldn't have let him make love to her. Couldn't have borne it if he'd discovered the truth—which he would have. Couldn't have borne the humiliation.

Let him think she'd been out for revenge the whole time. It was better that way, better than admitting that there was something wrong with her, that she was some kind of freak.

Halfway back sat the ancient throne carved from rock, its cool granite warming under the rays of the morning sun. She glanced at her watch, found it still early, so she sat herself down on the weather-worn seat that looked out to sea, her fingers absently drinking in the texture of the smooth stone while she watched the Genoa ferry disappearing into the distance.

Twenty-nine and still a virgin. Why couldn't she have done it, just once? She'd had boyfriends. She hadn't exactly lived the life of a nun. And there were at least a couple of guys in her design classes who weren't gay and who didn't already have girlfriends. She could have easily slept with one of them, surely? There'd been enough invitations, enough parties fuelled by cheap wine and loud music.

She could easily have let herself. But what would it have meant?

Nothing but sex. She'd always wanted more than just sex. She laughed as she looked out to sea, watching the ever-shifting cloud of sea birds atop Iseo's Pyramid. Rafe had always accused her of being a romantic.

Love and sex. Sex and love. Was it so hard to want them together?

Besides, it wasn't as if she'd planned to remain a virgin until the ripe old age of twenty-nine. It was just the way it had happened. If she'd had her way, she wouldn't have been a virgin at seventeen.

A failed seductress at sixteen. A failed lover at twenty-nine. The way she was going, she'd still be a virgin aged ninety-nine. What would the tabloids and magazines make of that? Already she could see the headline: *Princess Marietta—Eternal Virgin*. And for all the sensationalist reporting of celebrity and royalty love affairs, the real sensation would be that someone had managed to remain a virgin so long.

The stone warmed her jeans and the flesh beneath, reminding her of another warmth, another heat. And most of all, of an uncomfortable need. And despite knowing she'd done the right thing in throwing Yannis out last night, part of her wished things had been different, that they'd made love and put an end to this interminable wanting.

What did that say for her romantic soul? She hadn't been worried about love last night. It had all been about the sex. About sheer animal lust.

She'd just picked the wrong man to fall in lust with.

The ferry was long gone, its foaming wake swallowed back into the blue, blue sea when she finally stood. The sun was getting hot, and without a hat she would burn, the curse of inheriting her mother's fair colouring. She could live with that. She just wished she hadn't had to inherit the curse of her mother's failed love life. What was wrong with them that they both had to fall in love with the wrong man, her mother with a prince who, already with a legitimate heir and a spare, didn't need another woman breeding his bastard children, and she, who'd let a teenage crush and romantic notions stifle her life?

She'd already started back when she saw him, a man running towards her, calling out to her, a phalanx of the palace guard at his shoulder. She squinted against the sun. Sebastiano? But why? What was going on?

'What is it? she asked as they drew close enough to hear her, most of the guards streaming past her down the path beyond, four guards remaining with her brother's *aide-de-camp*. 'What's wrong.'

Sebastiano came to a stop, his hand on his chest as he breathed long and hard, gasping for air. 'Princess Marietta,' he gasped, 'Prince Raphael has been sick with worry looking for you. You must come back to the Castello…' he took another raggedy breath '…at once.'

'But why?' she asked, even as he turned and started back towards the apparent safety of the ancient walled castle. 'What's happened?'

'The Prince will give you the details. As soon as we are safe within the Castello walls.'

'Safe? What are you talking about?'

'You must hurry, Princess.'

'You can't tell me why?'

'Please,' he insisted, 'You must hurry. You may be in danger out here.'

So much for never seeing Yannis again. Her already racing heart took a jolt when she entered the library. For he was there, standing by the window as she entered, his arms crossed, his features unreadable in the wash of light from behind, but she didn't have to see his face, she could read his anger in his stance.

'Where the hell have you been?' His voice boomed out across the room. 'The entire palace has been looking for you.'

She crossed her arms, fighting the impulse to turn around and walk right out of there again. 'Sorry to put you out. I went for a walk. I didn't realise I should have asked your permission.' And then, because she knew she sounded churlish, she tempered her attack. 'Anyway, what's going on? Sebastiano said there's some kind of danger.'

'Yannis was just worried about you, as we all were.' Her brother's voice cut through the tension in the room, and her focus widened, her eyes adjusting to being inside. Yannis had been the first person she'd noticed, maybe because he was standing against the window, sucking up the light. But now she realised her brother and his new wife were also there, sitting together on a low chesterfield, Sienna's eyes pinched, her hands cradled in her new husband's.

The injustice rammed home to Marietta. Whatever

was happening, whatever danger there existed, had eaten into what should be their honeymoon, supposedly a joyous time. It wasn't fair.

As she watched, her brother lifted one of Sienna's hands and kissed the back of it before placing them both in her lap and rising. 'You weren't in your room. We were all worried.'

'I was just out walking,' she said, much more reasonably this time now she wasn't being yelled at. 'Along the cliff path. I didn't mean to cause you any concern. I had no idea.'

'I know.'

'So what's going on? What kind of threat are we talking about? How dangerous is it?'

'Marietta,' her brother said, taking her arm and leading her to sit in the chair alongside the chesterfield, the dark cloud that was Yannis hovering behind. 'There's probably nothing in it. Probably nothing at all. But we have to take it seriously.'

'Take what seriously?'

Her brother took a breath as he chose his words, his look so solemn and sad that she felt the answering quake all the way to her toes. 'There's been a threat made against the royal family.' He paused a second before continuing. 'A death threat.'

Time stretched in the ensuing silence, pulled tighter and tighter, while dust motes danced on slanting sunbeams and the world beneath her slanted in parallel. 'A death threat?'

'And you were out walking on the cliff-top! What the hell were you thinking?'

Blood that had turned ice-cold with the knowledge of a death threat, suddenly ran hot. She hadn't wanted to see Yannis today. Or ever again for that matter. But if she had to see him, she certainly didn't want to hear him, or to be told how irresponsible she was. 'I didn't know! I certainly didn't go out there to make your life more difficult, appealing though that prospect is.'

Beside her, Rafe took her hand. 'Marietta, nobody is blaming you. But we have to be careful. It's probably just a hoax, but until the authorities can confirm that, we have to be careful.'

'I'm supposed to be leaving today.'

Her brother nodded. 'I know. Sebastiano and I have discussed it, and we think that's the best thing.'

'But I can't leave you both now. Not knowing there's this threat hanging over you.' She looked over at her new sister-in-law. 'How can you expect me to leave, knowing you could be in danger? It's not fair. You've just got married. You have the babies coming. You shouldn't have a care in the world.'

Sienna nodded but smiled up at her, 'It's not the way I would have chosen to begin my marriage, but I knew that such things were possible. It is a danger for anyone in the public eye these days, as you know yourself. But if it helps, Sebastiano thinks it may just be a bluff. I'm confident it will come to nothing.'

'But if he thinks they're bluffing—'

'We still have to take the threats seriously,' Rafe said, putting into words what Marietta already knew to be true. There was no way they could take any hint of a

threat lightly with the future of Montvelatte so perilously balanced. Nothing must be allowed to happen to
the new royal family and the babies that were so critical
to the continuation of the principality.

'The likelihood is that it's all a bluff,' Rafe continued, 'and the last desperate attempts of one of the former
Prince's cronies to destabilize the new regime. I'm sure
nothing will come of it.'

'And meanwhile, you expect me to leave?'

'Business as usual. Don't you have a gallery launch
to attend?'

'We could defer—'

'No!' her brother insisted. 'Remaining safe is one
thing. Curtailing our lives, crippling our lifestyles, is
another. To do so would be tantamount to giving in to
the threats. They need never act on their threats if they
cripple us with fear.'

'But if they do act?'

'Unlikely. Especially now we've been warned. Why
warn and risk increasing security before you make a
strike? So it's important that we go about our business
as per usual. With heightened security, of course.'

'So you still expect me to leave for Honolulu?'

'Business as usual,' her brother reiterated.

'Leaving you both here?'

'We have the entire palace guard to protect us.'

'I don't like it.'

'You don't have to like it.' Yannis's gravel-rich voice
was an unwelcome intrusion into her thoughts. This
was about family. *Her* family. He might be Rafe's best

friend, they might have grown up together as children, but that still didn't make him family.

'What's this got to do with you anyway?' she shot back, resenting the way he hovered in the background, intruding into the conversation like a snarling dog with a bone fixing for a fight.

'It's got everything to do with me. It's already been decided.'

She looked from her brother to Yannis to her brother again. 'What's been decided? What's he talking about?'

'It's the only way. You're going to Honolulu as planned,' Rafe said, 'and you have no reason to fear for your safety. Yannis is going with you.'

Shock punched the air from her lungs, then came back with a double blow that took her lungs out too, leaving her gasping for oxygen. Had her brother really just said that, or had she imagined it? Either way, it was her worst nightmare. Either way, it wasn't happening.

Logic told her she must have misheard. Whatever her brother thought had been agreed, there was no way Yannis would agree to accompanying her to Honolulu. No way in the world. He'd made it perfectly clear that he was happy to have nothing to do with her ever again, and he knew she felt the same way. Surely he would set Rafe straight?

But Yannis remained where he was, sullen and silent, the dark vibrations coming from him his only communication.

'I don't think so,' she said, when it was clear nobody

was going to come to her rescue. 'There must be some mistake.'

'There is no mistake,' she heard Yannis say in his most implacable tone. 'I'm coming with you.'

He had to be kidding. This was supposed to be a solution? Something that Yannis had agreed to? After what had happened last night, nothing could seem less likely.

'I don't need a babysitter!' she protested. 'You said yourself that it's most likely a hoax. I'll be fine.'

'You have to have protection, at least until we prove it either way. You can't go otherwise.'

'Then send Sebastiano. Or find someone else! Surely there's got to be someone in the palace guard who would enjoy a holiday in Hawaii?'

'Why, when Yannis is the obvious choice. Apart from his Greek army training, he's worked on some of our Hawaiian clients. He knows Honolulu backwards. And I trust him. You couldn't be in safer hands.'

She had no doubt about Yannis's fitness and strength—not if his muscle definition was any indication—and neither could she argue about his army training, knowing how every Greek man had to spend a year in the Greek army, but that still didn't mean she had to agree with Rafe's choice of a bodyguard. 'Surely Yannis has much more important things to worry about than looking after me. Isn't he in charge of all of your U.S. operations? How is he possibly going to manage all that from Hawaii?'

'Last time I heard,' Yannis interrupted, 'Hawaii was part of the United States.'

It didn't make sense. Anyone would think he wanted to take on this role. And there was no way that was possible. Last night the feeling had been mutual.

She shook her head, feeling herself in a whirlpool, being sucked down to a place she didn't want to go. 'I don't want him,' she said, quickly qualifying her words by adding, 'I don't want this. It's unnecessary,' in case anyone might think there was anything personal in her protest. 'Isn't there another way?'

'I know this has come as a shock to you,' her brother replied, 'but there is no other way. You can't expect to travel alone any more, you're a princess now. And even without any security threats, there will still be the paparazzi lying in wait. Life has changed for us, little sister. Perhaps not always for the better, but it is better to deal with these possibilities before they become problems.'

'Look,' she argued, clutching at straws growing shorter by the second, 'I have a hotel booked in Honolulu. I'll get it upgraded to a penthouse suite. Send me a guard and, together with hotel security, I'm sure I'll be safe there. There's no need for Yannis to mess with his schedules. It's too much to ask.'

'Yannis has already agreed.'

'But I'll be there for months. Six at least while the design studio gets off the ground. This is crazy.'

'Yannis will only stay while there is a perceived threat. Who knows, this could all blow over in a matter of weeks, maybe even days.'

But Marietta knew that even days would be too long.

The prospect of weeks spent in his company sent her spirits plummeting. She was supposed to be embarking on an exciting new phase of her career. Instead she had such a feeling of impending doom that she felt her entire being weighed down by it.

'Please, Marietta,' her sister-in-law said. 'We want to be sure you will be safe. Raphael could hardly trust anyone more.'

'I know,' she replied softly, knowing she could never be safe around that man. He shook her foundations, he challenged her body and soul, he turned her inside out with longing, with hate and a host of emotions she didn't want to put names to. Safe anywhere near Yannis? She didn't think so. 'It's just…'

'Just what?'

His voice sounded like a whip cracking in the room, but he was sick of listening to her, sick of hearing her pathetic pleas. Could she have laid it on any thicker? Could she have made it any plainer that she didn't want a thing to do with him? No on both counts.

Her eyes blinked up at him, the action failing to banish the moisture turning their surface to satin. 'Nothing,' she said, her voice no more than a whisper. 'Just nothing. I guess I don't have a choice.'

'No,' he confirmed. 'No choice at all.'

He left then, to make the final arrangements, the matter settled as far as it could be, a ball of anger at her protests pulsing like a living thing inside him. Did she really think he wanted to do this, babysit the woman who had teased him within an inch of being inside her before pretending that she'd changed her mind, pretending that she was somehow the victim in all this?

Not a chance.

He'd planned to be out of here today. Back to his office and his desk and the world of finance where no challenge was too great to overcome. Numbers, he could understand. Bringing the financially dead back to life was his forte. And, as a result, making money came as naturally to him as breathing, which was just as well, seeing he'd had to make a lot of it to pull his family from the nightmare that this woman had landed him in. A woman he wanted nothing more to do with.

Twice now she'd fouled his life. And now he was supposed to look after her? No one could have asked such a thing of him. Nobody but Raphael. 'Keep her safe,' he'd asked. 'I couldn't trust anyone else.'

He thought he could trust Yannis to keep her safe? That was a laugh when all he wanted to do was throttle her. She was the worst kind of tease, and the only possible pleasure he could get from this situation was that she'd thought she was home free.

Now was his chance. He'd make her pay for leading him on.

He'd make her pay!

CHAPTER SIX

Sienna called out to her as Marietta made her way back to her room, feeling heartsick, her spirits at an all-time low. She forced a smile to her face as the other woman caught up to her, asking if she could talk to her as she caught her in a shaky hug. The passageway ended in a large bay window with a sitting area to take in the view over the nearby cliffs and turquoise sea, and Sienna pulled her down next to her on the sofa.

'Are you okay?' Sienna asked, genuine concern in her voice. 'You seemed so adamant back there.'

'I'm sorry,' she said, feeling contrite for the way she'd argued when all anyone was doing was trying to ensure her safety. 'I was just taken a bit by surprise.' A massive understatement, but at least it held more than an element of truth.

'I know. It was a huge shock to us all, although sadly it seems like such security concerns are par for the course these days. Though I hate to think there'll be a time when we're used to them.'

Her sister-in-law's words were so honest and true that Marietta suddenly felt guiltier than ever. Her brother's new wife was pregnant, expecting twins just a few short months from now, and she had to be worried sick about what she'd got herself into. She'd not been a princess a full day yet, and already threats had been made against the first family.

And yet all the while, Marietta had been more concerned with having to spend time with Yannis than with the real problem—a threat made against her family. She took Sienna's hands in hers, appalled at her own selfishness. 'I hate the thought of leaving you at a time like this. It doesn't seem right. Will you be all right?'

Colour lit the other woman's cheeks, her eyes shining bright and her smile radiant. 'I have Rafe to look after me. It might sound strange, but I've never felt safer. This is where I belong, at Rafe's side.' And her words warmed Marietta's frozen heart. 'But you,' Sienna continued, concern clouding her eyes. 'Will you be all right with Yannis?'

The question took her by surprise, and she felt her own colour rise in response. 'Of course,' she said, with false enthusiasm, 'why wouldn't I be?'

Sienna didn't look convinced. She sat there, shaking her head. 'This is all my fault.'

'What's your fault?'

'I know you told me he treated you like Rafe's little sister, but last night…'

'What about last night?'

'Well, it's just that someone saw you both out on the terrace.'

'Oh…it was after the dance,' Marietta explained in a rush. 'I needed some air.'

'So you didn't kiss him?'

Marietta cursed silently. Why had she let it happen? Of course someone would have seen. And of course the news would have filtered back. It was pure luck that there weren't pictures splashed all over the celebrity magazines with everyone these days having a camera in their phone. She shrugged. 'It was just a kiss,' she lied. 'For old times' sake.'

'Marietta, I'm so sorry, I thought it would be the perfect solution. When Rafe suggested Yannis, I supported him one hundred per cent. I would never have done that if I'd thought…'

'It's okay,' Marietta said. 'Really.' Because she couldn't blame Sienna at all, not when she'd been the one too weak to resist Yannis's advances, the one foolish enough to kiss him in public. She might as well have looped this particular noose around her own neck.

'How can it be okay? Just now it seemed like you were so angry with him, and he with you. At first, I thought he was angry because he'd been concerned about finding you. He was frantic when it was discovered you weren't in your room. But there was more to it than that, wasn't there? There must be more to it. Did something happen last night?'

Yannis had been frantic? That was a turn-up. She would have expected him to have been relieved that she was gone. But as for whether anything had happened last night... 'It was a misunderstanding, that's all. I think we're both sorry.'

'But now we've arranged for you both to go to Hawaii together.' And Sienna looked so genuinely remorseful that Marietta couldn't help but feel bad. 'I feel so foolish now. And to think I'd been hoping...'

Marietta stiffened. 'What were you hoping?'

'Nothing,' she said, with a shake of her head. 'Silly romantic stuff. Must be the wedding and everything getting to me.'

'No, tell me.' *Even though she knew.*

Sienna shrugged. 'When I heard about you both out on the terrace, I thought how nice it would be if you two hit it off after not seeing each other for so long. I would have loved for something like that to have happened at our wedding.'

Marietta gave a wan smile. What would her new sister-in-law say if she knew that the way they'd intended to hit it off last night had involved one short night of sex and a promise never to see each other again? 'Very romantic, although I can't see anything happening on that score. I have no marriage plans and Yannis is a confirmed bachelor. He's too busy being married to his career.'

'Though he must have entertained the idea at one time. Wasn't he engaged or something?'

'Yannis?' Marietta shook her head. 'Not that I've heard. Unless it was in the last few years.'

'No, not recently. I'm sure Rafe said something about

it being a long time ago, when they were both in their early twenties.' She shrugged when Marietta continued to offer no help. 'No matter. Maybe whatever happened then is half the reason he's so focused on his work. Rafe said he's driven.'

'Maybe,' Marietta agreed, mulling over Sienna's words and deciding she must have her wires crossed. Yannis had been like part of their family. She would have known if he'd been thinking of getting married, surely.

'Anyway,' Sienna continued, 'I just wanted to make sure you were all right. That I hadn't done the wrong thing by suggesting Yannis could look after you.'

Marietta gave her a squeeze. 'It'll be okay,' she said, with a conviction she didn't feel. 'It'll be fine.'

It wasn't. They met at the helicopter, their bags already stowed, the pilot ready for departure, on a day when the sun burned bright and hot above and the atmosphere was cold and frosty below. At least in the space surrounding Marietta and Yannis.

He didn't want to look at her, she noticed on the brief times he strayed into her gaze, his jaw stiff and set as he barked out orders, his eyes masked by sun glasses that didn't hide the resentment that simmered so close under that take-charge facade.

This wasn't the escape she'd had in mind when she'd dreamed of getting away from Montvelatte. She rubbed her bare arms as the helicopter lifted off and spun around before heading out over the blue, blue sea. This was escape into purgatory. Into a world where heaven seemed all too elusive and hell seemed all too close.

Still, she managed a smile as she waved to Sienna and Rafe, flanked as they were by a phalanx of the palace guard, as the ground below shrank and fell behind. Sienna had enough to worry about. And maybe Sebastiano was right. Maybe it wouldn't have to be for too long. At any time the threat could be proven to be a hoax, and Yannis could forget about protecting her and would be off back to New York or wherever it was where he could get on with the business of running the financial world instead.

There was supposed to be a silver lining to every cloud—or so they said. She settled back into her seat as the helicopter whumped its way across the sea to the plane that was waiting to take them to Hawaii. She would just have to wait for hers to become apparent.

The cool white house was more like a mansion, sprawling low and wide across the massive block, palms and frangipani trees disguising its full dimensions with splashes of vivid green. The limousine waited, engine idling, as the wide electronic gates slid slowly open.

'This is it?'

'This is it.'

'I would have been quite happy in the suite I had booked. There was no need to cancel it.'

'A hotel is open to the public, you would never have been safe there.'

'I could have booked additional security.'

'What? Like rock stars, immediately alerting everyone that a celebrity is staying? Not likely. You'll be much safer staying here.'

She looked out the window up at the massive house, unconvinced. It still looked like overkill to Marietta, a rambling mansion when a hotel room or even an apartment would have done perfectly well, just as a normal-sized car would have been perfectly adequate instead of this over-stretched limousine, but she hadn't won that argument and there was no point debating this one.

Far better to save her energy for the battles to come because, sure as hell, they would come.

She blinked eyes weary from too many hours spent in air-conditioning and a body clock turned upside down. First-class made international travel more comfortable, it was true, but it made no difference to the journey time. After more than a day in transit, Sienna had been more than ready to get off the plane. The humidity had hit her like a brick when she had. Around her neck the orchid lei the driver had presented her with on arrival felt heavy and hot, its otherwise sweet scent almost too much for her strung out senses.

At the far end, Yannis sat relaxed, his long legs stretched out and eating up the carpeted space between them. He looked cool and urbane, having shed his jacket and rolled up his sleeves—another reason to resent him, so she turned her head away, preferring to take in her new surroundings.

The car proceeded along the paved driveway lined with low unfamiliar shrubs and cool inviting lawns, the house sprawling before them. This close she could see the house's true dimensions. Not so low, now she was close, the double-storey home welcomed them with a massive portico under which the car came to a halt.

Steamy air met her as she alighted, so different to Montvelatte's crisp, clean air, though it was cooler here than at the airport, the temperature moderated by the shaded gardens and a gentle sea breeze. That breeze lifted the ends of her hair and tugged at her senses. And whereas Yannis made his way directly towards the enormous timber front doors, Marietta followed the lure of the breeze, catching a glimpse of vivid blue through an archway.

Different scents met her from this perfumed garden. Sweet tropical scents of hibiscus and frangipani all carried on the fresh sea air, the sound of the whoosh and suck of the ocean pulling her on until its green-blue brilliance stopped her in her tracks.

The house had absolute beach frontage, the skilfully tended lawns giving way to a fringe of palms, beyond which lay the beach in all its natural glory, stretching into the distance in both directions. Far down the coastline were the tall buildings and hotels that lined Waikiki's crowded beach, but there was no sign of highrise hotels and crowds here. Instead the beach was private, empty and unspoilt.

On impulse she dropped her bag and kicked off her shoes, feeling the shell-grit beach sand warm her feet.

'What are you doing?' Yannis's voice rang out from behind her. She lifted a hand and waved his concerns away without bothering to turn around. Wasn't it obvious what she was doing?

The water rushed up to her feet, swallowing them in a deliciously cool bath, before sucking at them, pulling them deeper into the sand. She sighed. It felt so good. She splashed along the shore, holding up her skirt. Maybe she should get her swimsuit and come back. Tomorrow she would meet up with Xavier and check on progress with the gallery. There was so much to do in the next two weeks before the launch that she might not have much of a chance to enjoy such simple pleasures. And surely there could be nothing better than a swim to freshen her up after the long flight.

The next wave rushed in, taking her unawares and splashing her up to her knees. She laughed and jumped back, straight into Yannis's hard-packed body.

She panicked, stumbling away from the electric shock of the contact, feet already unsteady from the long-haul flight doubly unsteady on sodden sand and with the sucking tide. Hands on her arms stopped her tumbling into the next wave, pulled her back from the foaming water, although there was no saving her skirt. It caught the full brunt of the wave and was drenched, the light fabric bunched and clinging to her legs like seaweed.

'What do you think you're doing?' he blasted when she was upright and relatively stable again.

She shrugged out of his grip.

'Having fun,' she shot back, battling to get her breathing under control. 'Maybe you should try it some time.'

'You're soaking.'

'I'll dry.'

'I wanted to show you the house.'

'Is the house going anywhere?'

'No.'

'Then I'll see it when I come in.'

'I'm supposed to look after you.'

She sighed and looked pointedly up and down the empty beach. 'Listen, Yannis, I realise you take your babysitting duties seriously, and I appreciate it— *really*—but does it look like I'm in any danger here?'

Only in danger of sending his blood pressure into orbit. Her wet skirt clung to her in a way that should be illegal, moulding to her long legs lovingly, perfect legs that he'd lain between, so close to pressing himself home. His groin ached at the thought.

'You have no concept.'

'I'll risk it.'

Her feline eyes sparked defiantly, her feet planted wide in the sand, the challenge clear. She would come when she was good and ready, and not before. Fine. He would leave her here to splash around in her clothes like a child, and he would select a room for her, preferably somewhere as far away from his as possible.

There was an unbelievable amount of work still to do. Marietta tried to blame her disappointment on jet lag and a restless night's sleep, but nothing could disguise the fact that the fit-out in the swanky Kalakaua Avenue store that was soon be the home of Paua International was nowhere near complete, and that the list of RSVPs that had accepted invitations to the opening was perilously short of the A-list VIPs who would guarantee the kind of press coverage they needed to really make a splash.

The only thing that kept her from a deeper feeling of depression was that Xavier, her partner, was already wallowing in that rancid pool. And from where she was standing, there simply wasn't room for both of them.

'So the contractor says they'll be ready?'

Xavier winced and nodded uncertainly. 'They said they *should* be.' Around them the shop front looked like a bombsite, with unfinished panelling and gaps in the walls from where bunches of electrical cables protruded. A scant fortnight from now they were supposed to be hosting a launch for two hundred guests and displaying jewellery worth millions in cases that were, so far, non-existent.

Neither of those options looked likely to happen at the moment, let alone both of them, despite Xavier's assurances that everything had been on track when she'd left Auckland for Rafe's wedding.

In reality, the only positive thought she had was that it was lucky she hadn't stayed on Montvelatte any longer. But if nobody showed up, what was the point, even if the contractors did manage to pull off a major miracle and get this shopfront somehow ready for business?

'Why aren't they accepting?' she asked, looking at the list that seemed way too short for so close to an event that had already garnered some good press. But it was the bang of a successful launch that would really kick-start the business, the resultant publicity sending people curious to see the latest Honolulu hot spot.

'What's the hold up? The date was checked and double-checked. There's nothing else big happening in Honolulu that night. How can we have a launch if nobody bothers to come?'

Xavier looked small in the spare lighting of the unfinished store, even before his shoulders sagged. 'Duke Kameāloha is the key. Apparently, without his acceptance, others will stay away in droves.'

Marietta was familiar with the name of the Hawaiian surfer turned singer turned politician, although she'd never met the man. Charismatic, coffee-skinned and popular beyond belief, he turned politics into a rock concert wherever he turned up. They had to have him. 'How can we ensure he comes?'

'I don't know,' Xavier admitted, looking suddenly frail and older than his fifty years. 'But unless we do, we might as well tell the contractors not to bother completing the fit-out.'

She rested one hand on his arm. Xavier had invested everything he had into launching this new operation, and she'd supported him all the way. If it didn't go well, it would break him. There was no way around it. The launch *had* to be a success.

'No, it won't come to that. It will be a success, you'll see. This gallery will be the biggest thing to hit Honolulu since the hula hoop.'

Her weak attempt at humour was completely wasted. Xavier merely frowned, his high brow crumpling with concern.

CHAPTER SEVEN

THE next few days were enough to make her doubt her own words. Acceptances were still only dribbling in, and at this stage it looked as if they wouldn't even need to bother with the caterers. Finger food for two hundred for a gathering of barely twenty? Definitely overkill.

And no matter how many times she called Duke's office, asking to speak to the man himself, she only ever received a terse, 'He'll get back to you.'

He never did.

Day after day blew by, with nothing to show for it but an increasing stress level. It was all too frustrating. The fit-out was progressing too slowly, the caterers were anxious for final numbers, and to top it all off, a phone call from Auckland had informed her that half her jewellery designs set for the launch were stuck in customs.

And it didn't help that every time she turned around, Yannis was there. Watching what she was doing, checking out who she was talking with, and generally getting in her way. It wasn't as if she felt she was in danger and needed a bodyguard. There'd been no hint of danger since they'd arrived, no news from Montvelatte to suggest that the threats were real, and still Yannis was there, like a dark shadow. Watching. Waiting.

It was so bad, she couldn't move without Yannis demanding to know where she was going and what she was doing. No wonder her head hurt. No wonder her sleep was suffering.

She stepped out of the doctor's consulting room, a prescription in her hand, only to find Yannis waiting for her.

'You don't have to follow me everywhere, you know,' she said, when she'd paid the receptionist and they'd stepped out of the cool air-conditioning of the clinic.

'I'm supposed to be looking after you,' was his comeback. 'How can I do that if you keep trying to slip away all the time?'

'It's only just around the corner from the gallery! It's not like I'm making a run for it.'

'Good,' he said, opening the limousine's wide door for her so she could slide into the passenger seat. 'Because it wouldn't do you any good. You wouldn't get far.'

'Is that a threat?'

He flashed a deadpan look at her that not even his dark glasses could disguise. 'Consider it a promise.'

He guided the car into the early evening traffic and headed back towards Kahala, and frustration got the better of her.

'Aren't you bored doing this?'

'I never get bored driving.' As if to prove his point, he shifted gears, harnessing a throaty power that had them smoothly overtaking a slower-moving car in front.

'You know that's not what I meant. You're supposed to be out saving the world from financial disaster. Not stuck here in Hawaii protecting me from something that's probably never going to happen.'

'Who says it's never going to happen?'

'You don't think there's any substance behind that threat, do you?'

'It doesn't matter what I think. This is what your brother asked me to do, and this is what I'm doing.'

'And if I asked you to leave?'

'No dice. I happen to have a healthy respect for your brother, Princess. I'm not about to let him down.'

'And it doesn't matter what I want?'

There was a momentary pause before he turned his head her way. 'What do you want, Princess?'

The wind was in his hair, tugging at the thick waves and making them move in a way her fingers itched to feel, muddying her thoughts until she wasn't sure of anything any more. 'I want…I want you to go away.'

'Oh, I plan to,' he said, and her spirits found instant respite. For whatever hassles she faced with the launch, how much simpler life would be if only he was gone!

And just as she was beginning to enjoy the prospect, he smiled at her. 'Just as soon as word from Montvelatte says I can.'

She thumped back into her leather seat, her spirits dumped on again, her hand at a pounding head that refused to let up. She pushed the button to open her window. Maybe fresh air was what she needed, not air filled with the smell of leather and machine and his unique scent.

He looked her way. 'What's wrong with you, anyway? What did the doctor say?'

'Strangely enough she said I'm stressed. I can't imagine why. She's given me sleeping tablets.'

'Good idea,' he came back with. 'You could do with a decent sleep. Just lately, you look like hell.'

'Why don't you say what you really think?'

'I was just saying—'

'Then don't. All right? Just don't.'

She couldn't wait for the car to pull into the driveway. Couldn't wait to escape the car's too small confines. Of course she looked like hell. But she didn't care what he thought, didn't care what she looked like. All she wanted was to get away to somewhere unpolluted by his presence.

He followed her to the front door where she was already scrabbling through her purse for her set of keys. 'Allow me,' he said, inserting his key into the lock and pushing the door open in front of her.

She left him for dead at the door, making for the kitchen, dropping her purse down and pouring herself a long glass of water.

'That should make you feel better.'

She spun around. 'What are you now? A doctor? That's quite a list of qualifications you've got going. Financial saviour of the universe, bodyguard and now doctor. Is there anything you can't do?'

'Cook,' he admitted, 'but I can order in. What do you feel like?'

'Nothing. I'm not hungry.'

'You have to eat something.'

'And now you're my mother?'

He scowled as he leaned back against the marble kitchen bench top. 'You're overwrought. Maybe you should go to bed.'

'And maybe you should mind your own business and just leave me alone.'

He sighed as a weary uncle might do with a recalcitrant child. 'Marietta, maybe you should just take your sleeping pill and go to bed.'

'Why should I do what you tell me to do?'

'Because it's what the doctor told you to do! I'm just the messenger. Now be a good girl and run along and do what the doctor says.'

Her eyes flashed cold fire. 'I'm not a child. Stop treating me like one.'

'Then don't act like one!'

She spun away, his words stinging, the kernel of truth they contained rapidly growing into a mature tree. She *was* acting like a child, but then what did he expect? How was she supposed to act when she was being driven crazy by his arrogance? By his very presence? Somehow the man seemed to bring out the very worst in her in every possible way. Why else would she have thrown herself into that kiss that night on the terrace? And why else would she be forever sniping at him now? The man was simply infuriating.

Still fuming, she crossed her arms and turned back to him, prepared to moderate her voice and be more reasonable—more adult—if that was what it took to get through to him. 'Look, I didn't ask to be stuck here with you.'

'Fine. I don't want to be stuck with you, either. But you are here, and I'm stuck with you, so let's make the best of it. Now take the damned pill and go to sleep.'

She opened her mouth to say something, and he cocked his head, waiting for her next volley, but she thought better of it.

'Fine,' she said at last before issuing her acerbic parting comment. 'Sweet dreams.'

Sweet dreams? Not likely. Especially not after the text message and email he'd received from Sebastiano containing news that had dashed any hopes he'd harboured of an early release from his princess-minding duties. A second threat had been received, this time a crudely constructed note with letters torn from newspapers and magazines spelling out the names of those in danger. Marietta's name was listed there, alongside those of her brother and his new wife. 'When you least expect it,' the message had read, 'I'll be there in the shadows, waiting…'

There were plenty of shadows in the garden, and for the first time Yannis began to question his choice of this property. Yes, it was secluded and private, but that very privacy could shroud an intruder. From first thing tomorrow he would double the guard on the gate and have security on the beach as well to ensure no access from that direction was possible.

After checking and double-checking all the doors and windows in the house, it seemed for ever until he could get to sleep, and then it was in snatches, deep sleep eluding him but for brief tremulous dreams filled with pictures of a blonde-haired woman with no right to invade them.

She was driving him crazy. Did she really think she was the one with the rough end of the deal? He'd give anything to be back in his New York office again, swimming amongst the corporate sharks in his familiar financial pool. He knew how the sharks worked. He knew what made them tick. Figuring out what made Marietta tick was another matter entirely.

A noise roused him from his tossing and turning. At least, it could have been a noise. He lay there in the dark, with a prickle at the back of his neck and his senses suddenly on high alert, while his ears strained for any hint of a repeat of whatever it was that had snapped his senses to wakefulness. Outside he could hear the wind whipping through the forest of palm trees lining the shore, the whoosh of waves a constant. It was neither of those that had woken him, it had been something inside. Something out of place that shouldn't have been there.

When the sound came again, he was ready for it, his ears discerning a gentle bump and a scraping sound and then, not too long after, another, as if someone was moving around but trying to be quiet in the darkness beyond his room.

Sto thiavolo! If someone had broken into the house! And Marietta dead to the world. Whatever he thought of her, Rafe would never forgive him if anything happened to his sister while she was in his care.

He slid soundlessly from the bed and padded to the door, silently pulling it open so he could peer out into the dark depths. Something moved. A shadow in the gloom. Yannis pressed his back to the wall and pushed his way along it, creeping silently towards the living room. He heard a noise like a cupboard door being opened and closed, and then another, and his thoughts veered direction. If someone was after the Princess, surely they'd head for the bedrooms? But this sounded like someone was searching for something. A common thief rather than some other kind of threat? It was possible.

He found the intruder in the kitchen, a dark shadow, for the moment unmoving, something that jarred in his still sleep-blurred senses, but he already had his hand on the light switch and the advantage was his.

'What are you doing?' He snapped on the lights, already moving closer, determined to cut off any means of escape, when he recognised her.

She spun around on a gasp, the glass in her hand skidding out of her grip and launching its contents in an arc across the room. He was there in a heartbeat, but not fast enough to catch the glass. Cold water drenched his pyjama pants, the glass landing unceremoniously on his foot before skittling away unbroken across the tiled floor.

She gasped, her hand over her chest, her one concession to repentance before her eyes hardened to a crystal finish. 'What the hell do you think I'm doing? I'm getting a glass of water. Or I was. until you decided to descend into the room like a thunderclap. What were you playing at? You scared the life out of me.'

He reached down, picked up the glass, and placed it with a satisfying thump on the countertop.

'You were supposed to be asleep.'

'And you weren't?'

'I'm not the one who was supposed to take a sleeping pill.'

She kicked up her chin, two splashes of red staining her cheeks. 'Then maybe you should have been. Maybe then I could have enjoyed a glass of water without having the living daylights scared out of me.'

'You could have made it more obvious it was you.'

'Of course it was me. And let me tell you, I am so sick of not being able to move without you checking up on me. I can't go to a doctor's appointment, I can't get a simple glass of water without you sticking your nose in where it's not wanted.'

A growl formed in the back of his throat. 'You should have taken the damned pill.'

'And miss the floor show?' She turned around and snatched another glass from the cupboard, turning on the faucet and filling it. 'Not a chance.'

She should have kept arguing with him. She should never have turned around. Because now he didn't have her sassy mouth to focus on. Instead he was treated to the unadulterated view of her back, and the tiny scraps of pink polka-dot fabric she obviously considered pyjamas. One scrap she probably called a singlet, although it covered little of her back and left a tantalising scrap of skin bare below its hem, and the other comprised an even tinier pair of boyleg pants that skimmed the twin mounds of her behind in a straight line and left absolutely nothing to the imagination. She went to bed wearing that? She might as well have been wearing nothing.

He swallowed, his mouth suddenly tinder dry as a mounting heat evaporated every drop of moisture. His wet pyjama pants clung to him, pulling tight as his flesh swelled and tightened beneath them, and heat turned to fury.

Damn Marietta! She was doing it to him again. She wasn't naked in his bed offering herself to him, but she might as well be. What reasonable man wouldn't take a view like that for an invitation?

But while he could have reached out and taken her right now as easily as the water in that glass slid down her exposed throat, he wouldn't give her that satisfaction. Not after their last unsatisfactory encounter. Instead he took hold of her arm, spinning her around. 'What the hell are you playing at?'

She'd counted to twenty. Twice. She'd recited her times tables in her head all the way up to the sevens, and still she couldn't erase the sight of Yannis, his olive-skinned chest naked, his pyjama pants slung low on his hips. That would have been enough to freeze her brain and tangle her tongue, but the picture of Yannis with that wet fabric moulded to his body and clinging to his skin closer than any fabric had a right to, was one she was never going to forget, no matter how many times tables she recited.

Then he'd spun her around and rendered all attempts at forgetting useless. What had once been a naked body under wet fabric was now a naked, very aroused body under wet fabric. She paused for air, her glass held more firmly in her hand this time, while her brain battled for reason.

'What am I playing at?' she asked, her voice suddenly way too breathy. 'I thought I was getting a drink of water. Instead I seem to have inadvertently triggered off world war three. How far did you say we were from Pearl Harbor again?'

He wheeled around, pacing the floor like a caged lion. 'You know what I'm talking about. I don't make the same mistakes twice. I'm not crazy enough to try to sleep with you again.'

Her eyes opened wide, and this time she put the glass down because she knew that after that declaration there was no way she'd remember to hang onto it. 'Well that's interesting, because I don't remember asking you.'

'Don't you?' He came closer until he stood directly in front of her, planted one hand alongside her on the bench top, and glared accusingly into her eyes. 'Then what do you call these?'

He flicked a finger under the tiny shoestring strap of her singlet top, the sudden electric brush of his finger-tip sparking her flesh alight. She jerked back as far as she could, wanting the movement to disguise just how much she had trembled at his touch, and wishing away the swelling in her breasts even as she felt her nipples peak and her breasts grow heavy and firm. Damn the man's arrogance! It wasn't as if he was wearing a hell of a lot more.

'I call them pyjamas. So let me play this game and

guess what you call what you're wearing.' Accusingly she cast her eyes downwards and immediately wished she hadn't. Where once the fabric of his pyjama pants had been merely form fitting, now it was distended, the evidence of the erection beneath unavoidable. She gasped and looked back up at him, suddenly dizzy with confusion, only to see that desire echoed in his eyes. A glint lit their dark depths, and his jaw kicked into a predatory smile, and suddenly she knew that whatever game they were playing, someone had changed the rules while she wasn't looking.

He dropped a hand to the bench beside her, so suddenly that she jumped. 'Wha-what are you doing?' she whispered, her voice a mere shadow of its usual self.

'You walk around this house wearing next to nothing and you have the nerve to ask me that?'

He was close. So close that she could see every individual lash that surrounded his dark eyes. So close that his scent coiled and curled into her. She licked lips parched dry with the heat of his searing gaze and swore that she could almost taste him on her tongue.

And still she didn't know what he wanted.

'I'm sorry,' she said, her eyes on his mouth, on lips that hovered a tantalising few inches away. 'I wasn't thinking.'

'No,' he agreed, and even in that simple word she found a strange and fascinating pleasure in the shape of his mouth and the way his lips moved. 'I didn't think you were.'

He knew he wasn't. He should go. He should let her go. He knew she was a tease, that she played this game of advance and retreat so well, that she could tempt one moment and chill a man to his bones in the next.

But right now that didn't seem to matter. Right now she was here, practically naked in the kitchen, and he could smell the want on her, could smell the desire coiling up between them, tendrils hooking into his flesh, preventing him from moving.

'Why didn't you take the damned tablet?'

Her eyes were on his mouth, the tip of her tongue poised on her lip. 'I don't like taking drugs to help me sleep.' Her voice sounded breathy, containing a husky note that hooked into him and pulled him even closer. 'I wanted to try and fall asleep naturally first.'

'But you didn't.'

'No.'

Her voice trailed away, and time seemed to stall between them until the air was thick with waiting. Thick with wanting. His heartbeat thundered in his ears, a drum beat, primitive and untamed, and sending the blood dancing wildly through his veins until his erection bucked with it, demanding a decision.

'I won't make the same mistake again,' she promised, and he was so close to her mouth now that he would swear he hadn't heard a thing, that instead he'd read the words on her lips.

He growled, his lips brushing over hers. Sweet. Oh, so achingly sweet that her taste twisted like barley sugar into his senses, squeezing his chest so tight that it hurt to breathe in. 'No,' he agreed, knowing he wouldn't be responsible for his actions if she did.

He wasn't responsible for his actions now. She was tying him up into knots so tight he couldn't breathe with it, couldn't think straight under the weight of the conflicting forces that drove him on. The desire for revenge still burned strong, the need to make her pay paramount, both for what she'd done so many years ago and then also in denying him the sweet completion she had promised would be his that night of the wedding. And still he craved her like nothing else in this world. He hungered to fill her now, to push himself inside her and assuage the savage beast inside him the demanded to be fed.

Yet he was supposed to be protecting her. Another threat had been made against the royal family, the danger escalating, and here he was acting like a school boy tempted by his first taste of sweet firm flesh.

If only they hadn't received that second threat; if it had been a hoax all along, he could have taken her here and now and to hell with the consequences, but he was supposed to be protecting her. And how could he possibly protect her when he couldn't protect himself from the effect she had on him?

Chest heaving, he summoned every remaining scrap of restraint he could muster and used it to push himself away, lurching across the room.

'No,' he repeated. 'Make sure that you don't!'

CHAPTER EIGHT

BREAKFAST the next morning was unbearable. Marietta tried to stay out of his way, but it seemed every time she moved in the house or turned around in the kitchen, Yannis was there, dark and silent and brooding, his hand just beating hers to the refrigerator door, his body language making it plain that he enjoyed the encounters just as little as she did.

And she didn't want to think about him in the kitchen, let alone meet him there, not after last night. She'd taken half a sleeping tablet when she'd returned to her room, but it hadn't stopped the constant replays in her head of what had happened—*and what hadn't.*

He avoided her eyes, and she his, and together they managed to make it to the car without having uttered a word to each other.

It was only when they were waiting for the gate to slide open that Marietta felt compelled to speak. 'There are two guards,' she said.

'That's right. There's another one on the beach-front too.'

She frowned as the car pulled onto the busy road. 'But why? We haven't had any problems...' She stopped, her blood suddenly running cold despite the heat of the morning sun's rays streaming through the windows. 'Something's happened, hasn't it? Something you're not telling me.'

For the first time that morning, Yannis actually looked at her. 'Rafe and Sienna are safe, if that's what you're worried about.'

And Marietta let go of a breath she hadn't realised she'd been holding. At least she could relax on that score. But Yannis's words still held the weight of words unspoken. 'There's something else, isn't there?'

He nodded, his eyes back on the road as he skilfully negotiated his way through the peak-hour traffic. 'A second threat's been received.'

If the news that Rafe and Sienna were currently safe was a huge relief, the knowledge that a second threat had been made was a major disappointment. The risk hadn't diminished, it had escalated for all of them. And for her the disappointment ran deeper, for now there was no chance that Yannis would be disappearing from her life any time soon. How long could they continue to live this way, walking on eggshells around each other, resentful of the other's existence while at the same time cursed with an attraction that could come to nothing? And, like last night, being tortured when it hadn't.

He could have had her in the kitchen last night, right there on the bench top between the sink and the appliances. He could have taken her there, and she wouldn't have moved a muscle to stop him. He'd been so angry with her, and yet even in the midst of their enmity, he'd found the means to make her want him.

It was crazy, but somehow the man transformed her logic into lust, instinct to imperative, and, more importantly, her determination to resist him into desire. If it hadn't been for Yannis seeing sense at the last moment last night, anything could have happened.

She would have let it.

She looked over at him, troubled by a new thought curling its way uncomfortably into her mind. 'When did you find out about this new threat?'

'Does it matter?'

'You thought I was someone breaking in last night, didn't you?'

He shrugged. 'You were supposed to be asleep.'

'I thought you were just checking up on me. I accused you of sticking your nose in where it wasn't wanted.'

Another shrug. 'There was no danger. Why not just leave it at that?'

But she couldn't leave it. She'd assumed he'd been checking up on her. In fact, all along she'd refused to take his role as her protector seriously—after all, the threat was supposed to be a hoax, wasn't it?

But Yannis obviously took his job seriously. And when that second threat had come, he hadn't hesitated to investigate when he'd heard noises that shouldn't have been there.

What if it had been an intruder? She shivered. Yannis had scared the daylights out of her, and she had no doubt he could do the same and more to any intruder. Just one look at that bare muscled chest and anyone crazy enough to break in would be making an instant bee line towards escape.

In fact, a girl could do a lot worse than have someone like Yannis looking out for her. Warmth radiated out from her spine, sending tingles to her fingers and toes. There was something to be said for having her own protector.

'I was wrong,' she said. 'I'm sorry.'

'Forget it,' he said.

'No, I mean it. I've been awful ever since you agreed to come here.

'Marietta,' he said, his eyes this time leaving the road long enough to look straight at her, 'I told Rafe I'd look after you, and I will. I was just doing my job.'

He saw the telltale flinch in her eyes before she pushed herself back in her seat and looked away, and he almost regretted putting it so bluntly. But it was true. For the time being, she was his responsibility. He didn't want her being grateful or apologising for her behaviour. He didn't want any reason at all to resent her less than he already did.

He wanted her to act the way he expected her to, the argumentative tease who'd never grown up. He didn't want her apologising for her bad behaviour and her false assumptions, and he sure as hell didn't want any reason to like her.

It was better that way.

It was nigh on impossible to live with the man after that. Day after day passed in a relentless grind until Marietta felt as if she was going mad. Every night she took her sleeping pill, and she'd sleep, but it was heavy like mud, and every morning she'd wake up groggy and drained and in no way ready to face a new day. Not when Yannis seemed to occupy such a large part of it, draining her patience and what was left of her flagging energy.

And when he wasn't driving her to work or home again, he was always there, lurking in the background. *Driving her crazy.*

Even when he was armed with a laptop and was catching up on his own work, even then she would catch him watching her, or find him hovering close by her shoulder if she wandered too far from his eagle-like gaze.

She tried to focus on the organisation of the still un-finished fit-out, battling to keep up Xavier's spirits in the meantime, but the shadow of Yannis extended over everything she did.

And while the tension was still there between them, as was the sensation of heightened senses she had whenever he was near, the brief flash of warmth she'd had at having Yannis as her protector was gone, dispelled in the cold hard knowledge that he was just doing his job. It shouldn't have mattered, not when she didn't want him around anyway. But somehow, on a level she didn't quite understand, and wanted to explore even less, it did.

When the call came to advise her that the jewellery consignment had arrived, and she told them she'd be right there to check it out before it was handed over to the security specialists, she knew before Yannis had uttered a word that he would drive her. But today his take-charge manner didn't bother her. Even his brooding presence couldn't put a dampener on the relief she felt that the designs had finally arrived.

Opening the cases and revealing the jewellery within was like meeting up with old friends, it had been so long since she'd packed them. Against the padded black velvet backing the silver shone, the paua shell woven between the wire an ever-changing feast of every shade of blue and green.

'These are your designs?' Yannis asked over her shoulder, and she looked up, surprised to find him so close, the closest he'd been since that night in the kitchen. His proximity and his scent momentarily shorted her brain, making words impossible, but he didn't seem to notice, instead picking up a pendant sculpted from paua shell and lassoed in silver wire, in which was cradled a single, magnificent Pacific pearl. It was one of her favourite pieces, uniting the classic elegance of the pearl with the vibrant beauty of the paua.

'It's beautiful,' he said, with something like confusion clouding his eyes, and her heart swelled.

She was proud of her work, justifiably proud, and even the telltale tinge of surprise in his voice could not detract from the pleasure she derived in someone else recognising the beauty of a piece. Nothing was more exciting than unearthing the natural wonder of the paua shell and combining it to make something stunning and unique from the best the South Seas had to offer, unless it was to have made a thing of beauty that someone else could appreciate. Especially if that someone else had once expressed surprise that she even had a job.

She smiled to herself as she took the piece from his hands and replaced it in the box, securing the packaging, happy to know the shipment had arrived safely and all complete. Maybe it shouldn't have mattered, but having Yannis recognise the beauty of her work gave her a secret pleasure.

Exactly the way the still too short guest list didn't.

Back in the office the excitement of the shipment arriving was fading fast. It was two days until the launch, and while the gallery was making progress, the guest list had stalled. For all their gorgeous jewellery, without a celebrity presence, there would be no press coverage. Without press coverage, they might as well not bother.

Xavier deserved better than that. He'd invested everything in this new venture, his faith in her designs paramount. And yet the launch looked like faltering because of nothing to do with the designs. It wasn't right. It certainly wasn't just.

She hung up the phone one more time, feeling hope sliding away fast. Today, for the very first time, she'd played the princess card, something she'd promised herself that she'd never do. After all, this launch wasn't about her being a princess, it was about her being a jewellery designer. She wanted success for the business in its own right, not because of her sudden royal connections.

But the woman at the other end of the phone had been unconvinced, as if she'd suspected it was the last feeble attempt of a desperate woman who'd been turned down one too many times, which it was, even if what she'd told her also happened to be the truth. For just a moment, as Marietta replaced the receiver, she thought about calling back and telling the woman she could prove it, except there was no point; the woman had told her Duke was overseas and couldn't be contacted anyway. What hope did they have now?

Later that day she sat on the sandy beach in front of the house, flexing her feet in front of her and drinking up the late afternoon sunshine as the security guard kept discrete watch from the edge of the garden behind. Yannis had brought her home and immediately headed into the room he'd sequestered as a study to finish some business. And instead of changing into something casual, as she usually did in the evenings, she'd opted for a swim. It was still warm, the sun some distance from setting, though the rays were already slicing redder through the sky, and she'd thought the beach might soothe her soul.

And it was doing exactly that. The whoosh of waves along the shore, the call of sea birds, and the rustle of leaves on the early evening breeze were like a balm to her very being. After a day when her spirits had soared high with the delivery of the collection, only to be dashed again with the news that Duke was out of the country, and her attempts to contact him futile, she needed it more than ever.

It was so beautiful here. A different kind of beauti-ful from Montvelatte, where the dry salt air and hot summers gave birth along the coast to low-lying bushes and herbs with tiny scented flowers. Here the tropical air spawned vegetation lush and bountiful, with flowers bright and large. Closer to how Auckland had been, that most northern city in New Zealand, only more so. And all of them with their particular kind of beauty. The heat from the sun stung one shoulder, even though it was well past the danger period of the day. Marietta was reaching for the sunscreen when it was stolen from her grasp. She jumped, immediately assuming it must be the guard, only to have Yannis plop down onto his knees behind her.

'I heard you were out here,' he said. She heard lotion being squeezed from the bottle, not surprised in the least that he had the guards inform him of her every movement outside when he had her covered inside, less sure about why he should bother to join her. Then lotion met her skin and she gasped, and not only from the impact of the cold cream.

'You were busy,' she said, trying to sound normal. 'I thought I'd make the most of the beach before it got dark.'

He was smoothing the lotion onto her back, his hands making broad strokes from her spine to her shoulders and down her arms, and she was going to say it was probably unnecessary, that she had probably been over-cautious reaching for the bottle given the lateness of the afternoon, but she didn't.

Not when the first panic she'd felt at his touch turned to relaxation under his skilful touch. And certainly not when his hands turned the tension in her muscles into an altogether different kind of tension, a heaviness that pooled low and deep inside her. His thumbs made circles in her pressure points, and in spite of herself, her neck rolled with them.

'You're so tense.'

She laughed ironically. 'Tell me something I don't know.'

'But the shipment's arrived, and the gallery is looking good. I thought you'd be pleased with how it's looking for the launch.'

She shook her head. 'There still may be no point in a launch if we can't pull a big celebrity to attend the opening. Right now that doesn't look likely. We need someone of the calibre of Duke Kameāloha to turn up, and be seen to turn up, otherwise the whole evening will be a failure.'

His fingers stalled. 'So why not just call him up and ask him?'

'I have. Every day, probably a dozen times in all. And every time they've said they'll get back to me. Until today, when I learned he's out of the country, so there's probably no chance anyway. Right now it looks like we'd be better off cancelling the whole event rather than face the humiliation of no one turning up.'

His thumbs resumed, working some kind of magic on her shoulders. 'And if this Duke guy did turn up, it would make that much of a difference?'

'Apparently he's the number one hot property in Honolulu. If he appears somewhere, it's like giving it the official seal of approval. I can't even get television coverage for the launch without them having a drawcard like him to show up. It's crazy. We have a great product and a great concept, and I know we could do well if only…' She lifted some sand into her hand, made a fist of it, and watched it slowly trickle away, seeing the success of the launch trickle away with it.

'Surely anyone would be mad to say no to an invitation to meet a real princess.'

She slapped her empty hands together. 'I didn't like to mention it.'

Once again his fingers stilled before resuming their work. 'Because you didn't want to advertise it given the security concerns?'

'A little, I guess, although enough details have been printed in the press for anyone to make the connection. I just didn't think it was relevant.'

'You didn't think it relevant? You're inviting someone to a major event and you haven't mentioned the fact that you're a princess?'

She stiffened, finding criticism in his words. 'This launch isn't about Marietta Lombardi, the princess. This is about Marietta Lombardi, jewellery designer. The collection should speak for itself.'

'But if nobody comes, the collection can speak all it likes, it can even shout as loudly as it likes, but who will hear? Maybe it's time you let him know.'

It was way, way too late for that advice, even if she'd wanted to hear it. She shrugged. 'If it makes you feel any better, I did. I called his office again today.'

'And?'

'They didn't believe me.' She picked up another fistful of sand and this time flung it back down. 'Game over.'

Yannis snapped the top back on the bottle and sat down alongside her. 'I can't believe you didn't tell them earlier. It might have made your job easier.'

Marietta missed his hands sliding warm and luxuriously over her skin. She didn't miss the criticism in his words. 'I told you. This has nothing to do with being a princess. Jewellery design is my work. It's part of who I am.'

'But you're a princess now too. Don't you have responsibilities—to Montvelatte, to its people?'

'Yes, and those responsibilities don't involve using my position for personal gain. Or are you forgetting the previous regime and what brought them down?'

'Who's talking about personal gain? You're a princess; what's wrong with admitting it for some positive publicity? You're also promoting Montvelatte, then, at the same time as your launch. And if it's the difference between the success or failure of your new venture…'

He left the sentence hanging, and she was more than capable of filling in the blanks. Okay, so maybe he was right. Hadn't she determined that for herself when she'd decided to do just that? But she certainly didn't need to hear it from him. She already felt a failure. She didn't need to be reminded of how big a failure she was.

She'd let Xavier down by not allowing her royal status to be mentioned in any press releases, and in doing so she'd let the business down. Most of all, she now felt she'd let Montvelatte and its people down. Anyone would think she was ashamed of being its princess!

Abruptly she pushed herself to her feet, brushing the sand from her legs. She had enough lotion on her shoulders for a summer full of sunshine, and she was about to wash it all off. 'I think I might have a swim now before it gets too dark.'

It was nowhere near dark, the westering sun splashing red light against the layers of sky and casting ribbons of silver-red across the water beneath, but it was the best excuse she could come up with at short notice.

She jogged down to the water's edge, hesitating fractionally as her legs were embraced by the cool water of the Pacific Ocean rushing to meet her before running in deeper, plunging headfirst under an incoming wave.

Refreshing, cool salt water hit her sun-warmed body, instantly revitalising tired muscles and frazzled nerves. She needed this. She struck out, slow steady strokes that took her along the curve of the shore and away from the man who unsettled her like no other.

Below her, tiny fish darted one way and then another, sucked backwards by the tide before surging forward. She knew how they felt, being tossed one way and then another no matter how much effort went into moving in any one direction. When would this security scare be over? When would Yannis finally be able to leave so she could get her life back on some normal kind of footing? Because normal wasn't possible with Yannis around.

Everything was supercharged: her emotions, her

instincts, even her awareness of her own body. Even the simple act of having lotion rubbed on her back had set alarm bells ringing in her mind, even while other parts of her had been busy putting out the welcome mat. It made no sense. She didn't want to be this aware of her own body, not if it was going to mess with her head like this.

Fish darted towards a large rock on the sea floor and then flashed silver away as the rock sprouted legs and loomed upwards in a cloud of sand, heading straight for her. It wasn't a shark—her panicked brain had registered at least that much information—but still fear clutched at her heart at the unfamiliar threat. She reared back, thrashing to get away as the creature brushed her leg, heavy and solid, its body an enormous black shadow under the water, and she screamed. Something grabbed hold of her floundering body from behind and instinct told her it must be Yannis. Never before had she been so happy to know he had followed her. She allowed herself to be pulled around into his arms as she clung to him, her arms tight around his neck, her heart pounding.

'It's okay,' he said. 'You're safe now.'

And even while she felt safer just knowing he was here, she knew they weren't. 'There's something in the water,' she cried, desperate for him to understand. 'It touched me!'

His hand stroked her back as if he was settling a child who'd had a bad dream.

'It's okay,' he repeated. 'You just had a shock. It wouldn't have hurt you. It was just a turtle.'

His words filtered through the remaining panic in her brain. She released her head slowly from the sanctuary it had found in the curve of his neck. 'A turtle?'

'They come into shore in the afternoon, usually a little further down the coast. You were lucky enough to meet one coming up for air.' He angled himself and released one hand to point across the water. 'Look, there it goes.'

She looked to where he was pointing and saw the blunt prehistoric head of the creature poking out of the low swell, its large shell-covered body following behind, before it languidly submerged into the water again.

'Oh, my God, I thought it was… I thought…' She felt like an idiot. *Just a turtle.* Admittedly the size of a small Italian sedan, but just a turtle, nonetheless.

And then she realised where she was and the death grip she still had on Yannis, and she felt even more of an idiot. 'I guess you can let me go now, in that case,' she said, trying to unwind her arms from around his neck as nonchalantly as possible.

'I guess I can,' he responded, without making a move to do so. The water slipped around them, cool and fresh in the warm evening air, air that even now seemed to be growing warmer, despite the lowering sun.

She looked at him inquiringly. Droplets clung to the ends of his hair, his dark eyelashes clumped and thick, his five o'clock shadow rendering his glorious Mediterranean features even darker.

And the look in his eyes.

She shivered in his arms, suddenly aware of all the

places their bodies met, all the places where bare skin met wet skin, and of all the places that ached to do so.

And suddenly she didn't feel so safe after all. 'Yannis?'

He looked at her, and in his eyes she read his turmoil and the opposition, the desire and the torment, and she felt it move her: a subtle shift inside.

And then he blinked and looked around as if suddenly aware of their surroundings again.

'It's getting late,' he growled. 'We should go.'

He didn't understand it. He'd come to Hawaii charged with protecting her, and thirsting for revenge the first time he could get it, and yet here he was, just two short weeks later, not certain what he wanted any more.

From his balcony, Yannis stared out over a moon-drenched sea, his view framed by palms swaying in a gentle breeze that carried with it the scent of frangipani and hibiscus and another thousand sweet scents that made him think of women. One woman in particular.

In the past few days, contrary to everything he'd expected, he'd only found himself feeling a growing respect for the woman he'd longed would fail. Her work ethic he couldn't fault. Her skill was amazing; her designs had taken him completely unawares and for that he cursed himself. He was supposed to be good at research—and yet he'd not taken one step towards investigating her credentials. Simply assumed she was overstating her case. But her skills, like her commitment, were first rate. Even her ethics he had to respect, even if she might be committing career suicide by not acknowledging her title.

The way she'd tilted her chin up and pouted at him when she'd told him that a jewellery designer was who she was, first and foremost, and the way she'd insisted on not using her title for personal gain—this wasn't the person he'd assumed her to be, the shallow tease who'd never grown up. What had happened to her in the last two weeks, and what had been the catalyst for her sudden change? And even while putting words to the question made it sound ridiculous, a new question turned his spine electric: or had he been wrong about her all along?

He wanted to laugh out loud at the prospect, but the laughter wouldn't come, not when the picture he had of this woman now was so different to the one he'd harboured before. But how could he have got it so wrong? In the kitchen that night when he'd found her scrabbling around in the dark, and then tonight in the sea when he'd 'saved' her from her brush with an ancient turtle, he'd been so close to kissing her. So close to so much more. And she'd done nothing to prevent it. Nothing to stop him. Didn't that prove something?

Only that she was still waiting for him. Teasing him at every opportunity. Tempting him. But did he really believe that? His hands fisted at his sides, a hammer pounding at his temples.

If she were really that kind of person, wouldn't she be trying to come onto him? But she'd done nothing to lead him on. Nothing but simply be. Sitting on a beach in a blue swimsuit that made the most of her long smooth limbs and the fair skin that needed protection.

He'd been the one unable to resist picking up the bottle of sunscreen. He'd been the one who'd needed the excuse—any excuse—to reach out and feel that skin under his hands. She hadn't invited him other than merely by being there. How could he blame her?

He strode across the balcony, one hand rubbing the back of his neck. What was wrong with him? Twice now he'd had her where he wanted her, been seconds away from taking that which he'd been denied, and twice he'd walked away. And yet he'd come here with the intention of making her pay for what she'd done. It didn't make sense.

The waves continued to roll in along the shore, the stars winked at him from high in a cloudless sky, and while questions surged through his tortured mind, answers proved more elusive, always slipping away just when he thought he had them within his grasp.

One thing, though, was clear. Her business had to succeed, and for that the launch had to be a success. Because then, when this security scare was over, she would have a business to build and devote herself to. She would have a life here on Hawaii.

And he could go.

CHAPTER NINE

THE weather for the launch evening was perfect, mild and warm with just the hint of a breeze. The kind of night that made you yearn to be outside and breathe the air and feel the velvet night air on your skin. The kind of night Marietta prayed people wanted to venture out on and would. Outside the gallery, trunks of palm trees were decked with thousands of tiny lights stretching metres into the night sky and turning the strip fronting the gallery into a fairy-tale world, while inside was a buzz of last-minute preparations.

After her frantic efforts of the last two weeks, Marietta felt strangely surplus to requirements. With an increasingly sick feeling she watched waiting staff in white shirts filling trays with crystal champagne flutes, and catering staff strategically placing canapés and bite-sized nibbles around the room in readiness for the guests. The guests she feared would not come.

She cast an anxious eye around the room. The glass display cases had all been checked, the jewellery pieces displayed within arranged and rearranged to show them off under the dazzling downlights to perfection, and now there was nothing left for her to do but worry.

Worry that Paua International was biting off more than it could chew in thinking it could compete against the big boys in Hawaii. Worry that her vision for jewellery inspired by the paua shell and pearls this region boasted would never be able to compete with the Tiffanys and Cartiers of this world. Then she caught sight of Yannis, tall and masterful across the room as he consulted with Xavier over something, and the real source of her worry took human form.

It was Yannis who had insisted that they not change the catering arrangements, that if they had slashed the catering requirements to a fraction of that estimated, then word would inevitably get out and drive down numbers further. Nobody would come, he had argued, if they thought they were the only guests. And to her irritation Xavier had listened to him as if Yannis was the expert on such matters and knew what he was talking about.

And now he was consulting with Xavier again as if it was his God given right, his dark head leaning down as Xavier listened intently, nodding his head, the omnipresent frown once again creasing his brow. She sucked in a badly needed breath. This was her domain. Her world. Why couldn't he stay out of it? Could the man do nothing without irritating her?

Given the events of the last week or more, the answer was clearly no. He managed to irritate her when they argued, he'd irritated her when he'd rubbed her back with lotion. Even when he'd just rescued her from her brush with a giant turtle. He irritated her. He confused her. He wormed his way into what should be sleep-filled nights and invaded her dreams and rest.

It was more than a week since that encounter in the kitchen, and the visions that plagued her at night had only grown worse, with no relief from the mounting need that pulsed through her body like some beast searching for a way out. How many nights had she tossed in her bed as if she'd been flung around in the bowels of a ship on a storm-tossed sea? Too many.

He'd almost kissed her, and she'd done nothing to stop him. He'd almost kissed her, and she'd wanted him to. She'd wanted him to do much more than that. He could have taken her then, and she would have done nothing to stop him. She'd been powerless to resist, bowled over by a sexual force that had tangled with her defences and stripped them away as easily as he could have stripped her of her virginity.

And she would have let him.

And then two nights ago, her senses warmed up by languid strokes of his hands on her back, and wrapped in his arms in the foaming wash from the waves, she'd thought he might kiss her again. Once again, she'd wanted him to.

But no. After a look that had melted her from the inside out, he had abruptly let her go, and she had returned shivering and strangely cold to the shore, left with nothing but an overwhelming sense of dissatisfaction that it hadn't happened. That once again this ache inside her would know no release.

And she so needed release.

It was strange how she now held no fear of him making love to her and discovering her secret any more, whereas that night of the wedding when he'd come to her room, she'd clung onto his argument that her virginity was the reason he'd thrown her out of his bed. At the time, it had given her fear a solid foundation. But in hindsight Yannis's claim made no sense. There had to be another reason for what he had done all those years ago—a better reason.

She swallowed, dry mouthed, as she watched the two men heavily engaged in conversation. Why did he have so much to say to Xavier? She watched him point to something Xavier held, shaking his head, and she saw Xavier take out his fountain pen and cross something out before making a brief note, and her blood heated to simmering point. If she wasn't mistaken, that was the running sheet for tonight's launch Xavier was holding. In consultation with Xavier just this afternoon, they'd changed the programme, shortening the formalities so they didn't stretch an already thin audience. Those arrangements had nothing at all to do with Yannis.

She almost growled. He had a way of getting under her skin and making her itch from the inside out, and if that wasn't enough reason to resent him, now he imagined he had some say in the proceedings of a business that had nothing to do with him.

He looked up then, almost as if he'd sensed her gaze, his brow slightly furrowed, his eyes questioning, and she sent him a disapproving glare, already weaving her way between waiting staff towards them. He was playing with fire, thinking he had any say in the organisation of this event. She was already stressed out over the evening without interference from that quarter.

Xavier was already disappearing somewhere in the back of the store, no doubt on some errand Yannis had sent him on. 'What's going on here?' she demanded. 'What was that all about?'

Yannis refused to look cowed and merely flashed her a smile, his dark eyes glinting with what looked like a challenge as he hailed a passing waiter bearing a tray of champagne flutes. He took two and passed one to her.

'I don't want it,' she said. 'What I want to know is what you were talking about with my partner.'

He set down the unwanted flute on the nearest horizontal surface as he took a sip of his own, his eyebrows rising in approval. 'We were talking about how beautiful you look tonight. And you do. Very beautiful. I don't know if it's the dress, which is breathtaking enough, or whatever it is you've done with your hair, which is a work of art all on its own. Has anyone told you that you look like a high Roman priestess?'

She swallowed, taken aback, having expected anything but the speech he'd come out with. She'd selected the emerald silk dress for its classic lines and the superb drape of the fabric, its designer one of her favourites, but she didn't need Yannis telling her he approved of her choice. Not when she was trying to be angry with him.

'That doesn't explain why Xavier was making changes to the programme. What was that all about?'

He shrugged and gave that enigmatic smile once more. 'I was merely helping out, offering assistance where required.'

And the frustration of the last two weeks bubbled up into fury.

'Who the hell do you think you are? This launch is fraught with enough difficulties without you sticking your nose in. Can't you see how important this is to Xavier and me? It's got *nothing* to do with you. We don't want your assistance,' she hissed, keeping her voice down, aware of the burble of voices behind her that hopefully signalled the arrival of the first guests. 'And we certainly don't need it.'

'Is that so?' he asked, his eyes glimmering coldly over the rim of his champagne flute. 'In that case, I wish I hadn't said anything. I'll certainly make sure I don't interfere again.'

'Thank you. You might think you know all about the world of business, but this business is our world. The last thing we need is your interference.'

'Point taken. And now you might want to exchange that scowl for a smile, Princess. I think the television crews need to know where to set up.'

Marietta bristled as she turned. 'What cr—' The words died on her lips as the film crews carrying cameras and sound gear made their way into the building.

She turned back to him, some sixth sense telling her than he knew more about this that he was letting on, but he was already moving away, issuing instructions as if he was the one in charge. And he was. She stood there while

Yannis calmly but confidently issued instructions, and she watched amazed while everyone fell in with his orders.

Xavier emerged from the back rooms, smiling for the first time in what seemed like weeks. 'Isn't it fantastic?' he asked her, but before she had a chance to answer, they were greeting a flow of guests that turned from a trickle to a flood, and there was no time to find out what was going on.

In a matter of minutes the gallery had come alive with a swirling crowd of people, women in designer dresses with halter necks and shoestring straps, splashing colour and tanned skin around the room and screaming dollar signs with every shift of fabric and slide of silk. Men looked cool in sharp linen-blended suits that made the most of the vee of the masculine shoulder-to-hip ratio, oozing style. Jewellery glittered and sparkled, adorning every ear and throat, the occasional nose and navel, and the cameras drank it in.

And just when she thought things couldn't get any better, a stretch limousine pulled up out the front, and the gallery became a paparazzi playground as Duke Kameāloha appeared. She was ushered to the front of the store, the cameras flashing as 'the Duke' met the princess. 'I didn't know you were coming,' she told him in between poses. 'I tried to contact you many times.'

He bowed low and smiled his generous Polynesian smile, and she could see why people took to him instantly. 'I am sorry it took so long, Your Highness. You should have told me you were a friend of Yannis.'

And before she could respond, he had been snatched

away from her, and a microphone was shoved under her nose, with questions from reporters and television cameras aimed at her.

If the number of beautiful people present and the dozens of bottles of champagne consumed were any indication, the evening was an outstanding success. But it was the applause that accompanied the parade of Marietta's signature collection that sealed it. Xavier held her hand and squeezed as each piece was celebrated by the audience, and she could feel his excitement, feel it echoed in her own rush of pride.

And then the formalities were over, and the real party got underway. People hovered over the display cabinets, champagne in hand, while a ukulele trio played in the background, and outside the evening slipped deeper into darkness. Marietta and Xavier smiled and chatted and received the praises of the crowd. She knew the hard work was only just beginning, and that the real mark of success would be down to whether tonight's enthusiasm transformed into tomorrow's sales, but the indications were good, and Marietta couldn't help but feel excited. They could make this venture work. It could be a success.

And somehow it was all down to Yannis.

She was silent as they made the drive back to the house at Kahala, the night sky like black satin, Diamond Head a looming jagged shadow on their left. Duke's revelation had taken her completely by surprise, and it was no consolation that the night had gone so well. In fact, that just made it worse. Knowing their success was due in no small part to Yannis sent her even deeper into herself.

He didn't owe her a thing; he made no secret of the fact that he'd be happy if he could be gone from Hawaii and back to his real life for ever. And yet tonight he'd done something that could set the foundation of Paua International's business success. It didn't make sense.

'You're quiet, Princess. Aren't you happy with the way the launch went?'

She swung her head around to look at him, but not because of his question. Because she'd only just realised that at some point something had changed, and he'd stopped calling her Princess and making it sound like an insult.

He had his eyes on the coast road ahead of him, and for a moment it was his face in profile that occupied her thoughts, a profile as strong as the man who bore it, a man who had told her he didn't want to be here as much as she wanted him gone, and yet who had just ensured the success of her business. He looked at her then, making something tremble inside her, and her confusion intensified ten-fold. Along with her shame at how she'd treated him earlier.

'I owe you an apology.'

'Is that right?'

She cursed under her breath and turned her head up into the inky darkness, searching for inspiration. He knew damned well she had been out of order before. So typical of him not to make it easy for her. But then, why should he? She'd been the one to tell him not to interfere.

'You got Duke Kameāloha to turn up. Along with the cameras and five times the number of people we thought were coming.'

'Did he tell you that?'

'Not about the cameras and the crowd. But it makes sense. I told him I'd been trying to get in touch with him for a while, and he said I should have mentioned I was a friend of yours.'

Beside her Yannis raised his eyebrows, saying nothing.

'How do you know him? How did you get him to come to the launch?'

The car speared through the warm night, air catching at her hair, tugging at the ends.

'I did him a favour once, when he was moving from surfing into business. I gave him some advice.'

'It must have been good advice to have got him plus a cast of thousands and the television coverage.'

He shrugged. 'Like you said, once he was in the bag, the rest was easy. A few words mentioned in the right ears—the suggestion of what amounts to Hawaiian royalty meeting a real live princess…'

'You did all that?' She shook her head. 'And I accused you of interfering.'

She sat back in her seat, lifting her face to the heavens. 'You saved the launch. Without you the night would have been a disaster.'

He said nothing, just steered the car down the mansion-lined road, pulling into the driveway and pausing briefly while the heavy gates swung open before continuing towards the house.

'I'm sorry,' she added when it was clear he was going to say nothing. 'I was wrong.'

He brought the car to a halt outside the house, pulling

on the handbrake. 'Yes. You were. Oh, and I forgot to tell you…' He was out of the car and around to her door, and she had to wait for him to continue. She took his hand warily, curious to hear what else he had to say as he helped her from the car. 'I had a call from Rafe tonight while you were entertaining the crowd.'

Her interest piqued, she asked. 'And? How are they? How's Sienna?'

'They're both fine,' he answered, brushing her concerns away. 'But he wanted me to know they caught the perpetrator who made the threats. It was a hoax, as they suspected, nothing but threats made by an old colleague of the former princes who didn't like all the good press the new regime was getting.'

'A hoax.' His words stilled her, settling on her uneasily, something feeling not quite right about her reaction. She was happy knowing Rafe and Sienna were free from any danger, but still… 'Well, that's good news, isn't it?'

'It is good news. It means you don't need your baby-sitter any more.'

A lump settled inside her chest. 'You're leaving?'

'Tomorrow.'

'I suppose that's for the best.'

'Yes.'

She looked down to where her hand still rested in his. 'There's one thing I don't understand.'

'Which is?'

'Why did you do it? Why did you go out of your way to help me tonight?'

His mind searched for the answer to a question he'd been asking himself all night. *She was his best friend's little sister. He'd been asked to look after her.* But even as the words rose on his tongue, he couldn't give them voice, not because they weren't true, but because somehow they weren't enough.

He looked down at her, her hair now messed and loosened from driving back with the top down, one thick lock of blonde hair coiling down her neck, its pointed tip resting heavily on her collar bone, a question mark for a question he didn't know the answer to. Her cheeks were pink, whether from the drive home, the excitement of the evening, or the news his services were no longer required and she'd be free of him, he didn't want to examine too closely. And still her lips remained slightly parted as if waiting for his response.

If he didn't know she'd just spent the last twenty minutes in an open-topped car with the fresh night wind in her hair and in her face, he'd think she looked as if she'd just been thoroughly made love to.

The way she would look after he'd thoroughly made love to her.

And he answered the only way he could. 'Isn't it enough that I did?'

She smiled up at him, her beautiful eyes filmed with moisture. 'Thank you. You don't know how much it means to Xavier. And to me.'

Something inside him was tearing apart. She drove him crazy when she argued with him. She drove him wild when she taunted him with her little pointed barbs.

But when she smiled at him like that, it was like losing himself, like falling into an abyss.

'You're going tomorrow,' she said from nowhere, and his mind scrabbled for the connection. But at least this was something he did know the answer to.

'Yes.'

'Then can you do me one more favour before you leave? If it isn't asking too much, I mean?' And she dipped her head away, her cheeks flaring as if she was already embarrassed.

He took her chin in his fingers, lifted it gently until she faced him once more. 'If I can. What is it?'

Her blue eyes widened as she regarded him solemnly. 'Will you kiss me?'

CHAPTER TEN

THERE are times in a man's life when there is no need for logical thought. No need for reason. Sometimes instinct is enough to tell a man which way to go.

This was one of those times.

He dipped his mouth to her lips and knew before he'd touched her that he'd made the right decision. Knew with every fibre of his being that this was the right thing to do. And then his lips brushed over hers, and her lips told him the same thing. Once, twice, three times his lips made featherlight passes over hers, each time confirming the truth.

She wasn't getting away this time.

He deepened the kiss, moving into her, until she met him from breast to toes, her green gown curling around his legs as he pulled her even closer. She trembled under his mouth, but she didn't withdraw, didn't pull away. Instead she gave as good as she got, her hands at his head, holding him there, keeping him there to share his mouth, his breath, his taste. Her tongue danced with his, her teeth nipped at his lips, and she opened herself in a way that he could not help but fill.

And the kiss went on, a frenzied coupling that would have no end but one. 'Make love with me,' she whispered on a tropical breeze that carried the perfume of a thousand different flowers and the scent of just one special woman. And he knew that this moment had been inevitable from the moment their eyes had caught across a crowded Castello ballroom, and he sensed that this time was right for them.

His breathing already ragged, he shrugged her into his arms and carried her to the doorway, still kissing her, her arms wound tight around his neck. She slid down his body and nuzzled his neck as he searched for his key, turning his blood to lava so that he almost forgot what he was doing and took her right there, rammed up against the front door. But somehow he managed to unlock the door, and they stumbled inside, moonlight slanting through slatted window shutters, the shadows of the shifting palms and ferns turning the walls into a moving canvas.

He spun her along the passageway, never out of her arms, but keeping them moving, the dance of passion, while all the time his lips made love to her face, her eyes, her mouth.

And when he had her in his room, at last he let her go for a moment, letting the moonlight catch her features, as if giving her one last chance to change her mind while he pulled his jacket off, shrugged out his shirt, and tugged off his tie.

He hadn't expected her to do a thing, but without

taking her eyes from him, her hands went behind her, the sides of her bodice flapping down as she slid down the zip at her back. She put fingers to the straps and slid them down her shoulders before letting them go, letting the weight of the fabric pull the dress to the floor.

'*Thea mou*,' he said. *My goddess.*

And the naked hunger in her eyes was too much for him. He collected her into his arms, and his mouth was on hers again, open, hungry, demanding.

His hands spanned her waist, his fingers digging into her perfect flesh. She wrapped her arms around his neck, long arms like a silken noose that he wanted still tighter.

He unclipped the lace bra cupping her breasts, and she let go of his neck long enough for him to fling it away before his hands were there, filling themselves with her flesh, his thumbs tweaking her nipples until she mewed with pleasure into his mouth. She pressed herself closer, skin against sinfully sweet skin, while her hands were like quicksilver down his back, her fingers diving under the band at his waist, pulling him to her, and it was his turn to groan into her mouth.

She was like purgatory and hell and eternal damnation all wrapped up in the sleek satin skin of a siren. But she promised paradise too, and it was that paradise he was seeking. And then her slim-fingered hand rounded his thigh and touched him—there—and he almost thought he'd found it.

He pulled her high, wrapping her legs around him, and spun her around, clutching her to him in a heated, erotic dance, seeking something, some place where this aching need could be satisfied. He blundered almost by accident into the bed, his sense of direction shot to hell, shut down by the weight of his other senses. Taste. Touch. Need. Those things were all that drove him.

He dropped her down onto the bed, his forearms breaking her fall as she landed, his lips leaving her sinful mouth only that he might suckle those perfect breasts.

She was temptation in the flesh. And she was almost his. He dipped his head lower, toying with the sweet cavern of her navel as he swept away her tiny pants and lost himself in the heady feel and scent of her.

Kataplikti, she was a rarity, this one, unmanicured and all the more beautiful with it. And he knew it was a real woman he was making love to, not someone who had chosen to wax their sexual maturity out of existence.

He parted her lips and tasted her, and she bucked into his mouth. 'Yannis,' she cried, almost a sob, her head shaking from side to side. 'Please.'

And when he ignored her and suckled that tight bud between his lips, she screamed. 'Yannis. Now!' There was so much more he wanted to do. So much more to explore. But there would be time for that later. They had the entire night. But for now there was time for just one thing.

He had the sense to reach for protection before he released himself, his erection bobbing free, aching and so hungry for its own taste of paradise it was all he could do to sheath himself. He drew her closer, wrapping her legs around him, and knowing that this time there would be no halt. This time he would find the fulfilment his body craved.

She felt him there, felt the hot press of solid flesh, felt her internal muscles welcoming and wished him inside where nothing else would matter and all the mistakes of the past would be swept away, and everything finally made good.

She looked up at her Mediterranean lover leaning over her, his olive skin glistening gold in the moonlight, the muscles in his arms as tight as if they'd been sculpted, and his eyes—his beautiful dark eyes looking exactly how she felt. Crazy. Reckless and mad and wonderful.

I love you.

His eyes grew suddenly wilder, tension in every feature, and then he thrust and speared himself home.

She blacked out. She must have blacked out for she remembered no pain. Just the feeling of him filling her, consuming her.

And when she opened her eyes, it was to find his eyes locked on hers, dark with questions, struck with accusation, but filled too with more urgent things, and as she felt his body move within hers, she sensed with a woman's intuition she hadn't even know she possessed that it was already too late for him, and that there would be no turning back.

And that suited her perfectly. She wanted no turning back. She wanted it all. *And then everything would be all right.*

His hesitation could not last. His slow withdrawal became another plunge into her welcoming depths. And then another, filling her so tightly, filling her with pleasure.

He rocked into her, and the pressure built, the pleasure increasing as he took her higher, taking her to a place she'd never been and where there was nowhere left to go. Until nowhere became everywhere as she came apart, splintering into pieces around him as he pumped his own release, pieces that sparkled and twinkled in the moonlit sky before settling slowly back to earth.

He collapsed over her, panting, his lungs gasping, and even as she reached her arms up to wrap them around him to keep him close, she sensed that she'd already lost him. He reared up on a supernatural cry, half torment, half anguish, pulling out of her as if she was the last place he wanted to be, when she'd been all he wanted just moments before.

'Why didn't you tell me?' he demanded, his back to her, trousers being hauled and zipped up to cover himself. 'Why the hell didn't you tell me?'

She rolled herself away from him, exposed and naked and suddenly ashamed.

'I… I didn't think it should matter.'

'You were wrong!' he countered, one glance in her direction terminated as if she was too vile to even look at. 'You were wrong! All that time you were a virgin!'

He spat the word out as if she was some kind of freak. She rolled off the bed, feeling ridiculous still wearing her heels, knees barely supporting her as she made a dive for her clothes, scooping them up and bunching them in front of her defensively. 'Don't go thinking it was for your benefit!'

'That's not the point. You should have told me!'

'What for? So you could mark another notch on your belt? Or so you could throw me out like the first time?'

'That's not why—'

'That's what you told me!'

'I didn't want to hurt you!'

'Maybe you should have thought about that thirteen years ago!'

'Marietta, listen—'

But she didn't stay to listen. Instead she made for the door and ran from the room.

'Damn,' he swore, still not understanding but realising he'd made a mess of things. But why hadn't she told him? Why had she let him think…? Oh, God, what had he thought?

'Marietta,' he called, already following her when his cell phone rang. He ignored the first few tones—he had more important things on his mind—until he recognised the sound as his mother's ring tone, and it stopped him in his tracks. He looked down the passageway where Marietta had fled, wanting to follow her. But the sound held him captive. Wouldn't let him go.

Sto thiavolo, why would his mother be calling now when she knew it was past midnight here? Unless…

With a last fleeting look towards the stairs where Marietta had disappeared, and a sickening feeling building in his gut, he turned and picked up his jacket, retrieving his phone and snapping it open.

'*Ne*?'

But it wasn't his mother's voice that greeted him. It was his father's doctor who made the call.

Shock held him captive as he heard the news. Shock collapsed him onto the bed as he worried for his mother. But it was a sense of betrayal that fired his senses when he realised what he had been doing while a crisis in a hospital half a world away had been taking place.

Making love with Marietta. The very woman who had caused his father's descent into illness thirteen long years ago.

She was a fool. She'd thought it wouldn't matter, that between them they'd established some kind of relationship where the most important thing was what they could be, rather than what they were.

But she'd been wrong. So wrong. Marietta slammed her bedroom door and wrapped herself in a thick robe, covering both her nakedness and her naivety. And yet there was no covering her foolishness. She'd made a fool of herself with Yannis when she was just sixteen years old. Thirteen years later she was still doing it, at a time when she should have known a whole lot better.

Would she ever learn?

Tonight had meant more to her than the successful launch of Paua International. It was clear Yannis had wanted her—that night in the kitchen, and then the swim when she'd so unexpectedly encountered the turtle, had made his desire more than plain. He'd wanted her, she was sure of it. But on both those nights, just when she'd thought it might lead to something more, had at times feared it would, he'd held back and done nothing.

And yet tonight, when she'd least expected it given his

determination not to get involved with her, he'd done something that ensured Paua International would not sink without a trace before it had even got underway. And she had to hand it to him. He'd done nothing heavy-handed, like injecting funds secretly or having some ghost bidder order the entire stock to inflate early sales. He'd simply made sure the launch would be the success it could be, ensuring the business at least had a fighting chance.

And that had touched her in a way she hadn't seen coming. That he cared enough to call in a favour for her benefit. Why should he do that? Why should he bother?

Whatever his reason, that he'd done so had meant more than anything. And maybe that was why, in the moment as he'd been poised over her, she'd actually imagined that she was in love with him.

What an idiot she'd been. She had to be mad.

She swiped her eyes with the back of one hand as she headed for the en suite bathroom, fighting back a fresh batch of tears. She would not cry! She was angry, that was all. Angry with herself for being so naïve. She snapped on the shower, determined to scrub her body of every last trace of Yannis and his touch. Damn Yannis to hell and back again! What was his problem? So what that she'd been a virgin? What was the big deal? Her virginity was history now. Gone. And it had been Yannis himself who'd finally swept it away. Yannis, who was leaving tomorrow.

Good riddance to both!

The knock at the door and her name being called took her by surprise. She looked over her shoulder towards the door, away from the tempting spray of hot water and the steam already rising in the shower stall. How could she face him again? How could he expect her to? Then she caught her reflection in the mirror, took in the smudged mascara and puffy eyes and decided some things weren't meant to be shared.

'I'm busy,' she called, turning back, testing the temperature with one hand.

'I need to talk to you.'

Why couldn't he just go away? What did he think he was going to do—apologise? How could anyone say sorry for what had happened?

'I don't want to hear it!'

'Marietta, let me in. My father is dying!'

CHAPTER ELEVEN

HE LOOKED like hell, his face tightly drawn, a simmering tension in every move that he made. And his eyes looked lost. Holes so black she could almost feel his pain. 'I'm leaving now,' he said, and she realised only then that he'd changed into dark pants and a knit top that skimmed his perfect chest as closely as her hands had so recently done, his thick hair still shower damp at the ends. 'I'm on the first flight out. Will you be all right?'

As if he cared. She swallowed, still clutching onto the door.

'Of course I will.'

'You don't need to stay here if you don't want to. If you'd rather move into an apartment or hotel.'

'I'll work something out.'

'I've ordered a taxi. I'll leave you the car.'

'Fine.'

His jaw moved as if he was grinding his teeth. He glanced at his watch. 'I have to go.'

She pulled her robe tighter around her. 'Yes.'

He looked at her, his face a bleak mask while his ink-black eyes searched her face. Looking for what? And then his chest rose on a deep breath. 'Good bye.'

Without waiting for a response he turned away.

'Yannis?'

He turned his head slowly back over his shoulder. 'What?'

'I'm sorry about your father.'

It was as if a gun had gone off in his head. He stopped, the blood in his veins thick and clogged with thirteen years of hate. Thirteen years of blame. And that blood ran hot, searing the backs of his eyes, scorching his senses.

'Are you?' he said, turning slowly around. 'Are you really sorry?'

She blinked, the lips that had once tempted him beyond belief parting as she frowned. 'Of course. Why wouldn't I be?'

'Because you're the reason he's there!'

She reeled back as if she'd taken a blow to the head. 'What are you talking about? That's crazy. I've never had anything to do with your father. What does his illness have to do with me?'

He made a move to say something, one hand held up and ready to slash through the air to reinforce his point, when the sound of a horn blaring somewhere outside halted him. He checked his watch again and pressed his lips together before looking at her.

'It has *everything* to do with you!'

His mother ushered him into the hospital room, her warm face unusually tight, her hair greyer than he remembered. But once inside the room, it was the bed in the centre that held his attention, the bed surrounded by equipment and drips and flashing lights, the bed that contained the shadow of the man that was his father.

'Papa,' he said, taking one gnarled hand in his own, careful not to bump the needle taped into the papery skin. 'It's me, Yannis.'

His father's eyelids flickered open, one more reluctant than the other. 'Yannis,' he croaked through a half droopy mouth, 'my son.'

He squeezed his father's hand, shocked at how gaunt and weak he looked. He'd been prepared for this, he'd thought, but actually seeing his father lying there so frail and ill, listening to his strained breathing, was almost more than he could bear. 'Papa.'

'Your mother has missed you,' his father said, his voice little more than a whisper, but the accusation was there, and guilt sliced into him.

He flashed his mother a look of apology. 'I've been busy.' She smiled in return, and he welcomed the brief return of her dimples. He'd missed her smile. He should have made the effort to come earlier.

'You will kill yourself working so hard,' his father continued, his voice straining. 'And why? What for?'

Yannis squeezed his eyes shut. To earn back the fortune he'd lost. *To make amends for losing his family everything.*

Instead he said softly, 'You know why,' and his father frowned and closed his eyes, and there would have been silence in the room if not for the constant beep of the monitor the older man was plugged into.

And just when he thought his father must have gone to sleep, he sighed and opened his eyes again, and Yannis could swear they contained tears. 'You have been a good son.' And it was Yannis's turn to shake his head, and he tried to pull his hand away, but, suddenly, bony fingers tightened around his as his father found an untapped reserve of strength and refused to let go.

'A good son,' he insisted before his strength gave way and he relaxed his grip. This time, though, Yannis didn't try to pull his hand away. His father took a deep gasp of oxygen. 'Do you know what I have learned, lying here?' he asked through his twisted mouth, and Yannis frowned.

'Tell me.'

'That fortunes come and go, and in the end they mean nothing. And that life is short, but means everything. Do you understand me?'

Yannis swallowed down on a lump in his throat that refused to budge, at the same time facing a welling up of emotions he'd always thought under control. 'I don't know.'

And his father sighed again, a look of sadness overcoming his gaunt features. 'A long time ago, I made a mistake…' He paused and took a few more breaths of oxygen. 'A mistake you've been paying the cost for ever since.'

'It was my mistake,' Yannis insisted. 'It was my actions that lost you a fortune.'

'And it was your work that brought it back to me. But look around this room. What good is a fortune when you are facing death?'

'Papa, don't say that.'

'Why not, when it is true? But thank you, my son. You have done more than any son should ever have to do. But you have paid for the sins of your father long enough. Now it is time for you to live. And to give your mother the grandchildren she hungers for.'

He looked over at his mother, and she shrugged, her lips pressed together as she battled to stem the flow of tears from her eyes.

'You never said.'

She shrugged and attempted to smile. 'You were too busy.'

And he cursed himself anew. He'd always been too busy. Always too busy working. He'd thought that was what he'd needed to do. Paying penance for the mistake he'd made so long ago.

It had driven him, this need. This obsession to work and to make millions. It had become the reason for his existence.

'Forgive me,' his father whispered, in a voice too frail to be real. 'Please forgive me.'

And the tears that had been pricking at Yannis's eyes ever since he'd arrived finally found their release.

The phone call came three nights after Yannis had left. Marietta was running on empty, the ongoing press coverage of the launch and the clear success of the gallery the only thing keeping her going. If it hadn't been for Xavier force-feeding her sandwiches at lunch-time, she wouldn't have bothered to eat.

'We haven't heard from you for a while,' her brother said.

'It's been busy,' she replied, kicking off her shoes after another late night working. And it had. Orders were piling up; the number of commissions she'd received were staggering. And all on the strength of a successful launch that would never have happened without Yannis.

She felt a stab of pain prick the overwhelming feeling of numbness she'd descended into, and turned her thoughts away. It was better when she didn't think about Yannis, didn't wonder at his cryptic parting remark. It was easier when she felt nothing.

Instead she tried to force herself to concentrate on what her brother and his wife were telling her, trying to match the enthusiasm in their voices, and knowing she fell far short.

Things were good in Montvelatte. The security threat had been dealt with, and once again her sister-in-law could concentrate on the important things in life—her new husband and their babies. She was already showing, she'd boasted proudly to Marietta, her waistband expanding as their twins made their presence felt.

Marietta smiled into the phone. They were so much in love. At least she was grateful for that. And finally, when they were about to say goodnight to her, Rafe took the phone and asked, 'Oh, have you heard from Yannis?'

And she had to admit that she hadn't. He'd made no effort to contact her since he'd left. Then again, she wasn't expecting him to.

'His father died yesterday,' he told her, and her heart clenched in her chest so tightly she had to sit down. He'd accused her of having something to do with his father's illness—no—he'd accused her of having *everything* to do with his father's illness. Would that mean he held her responsible for his death? But how? What had she done?

'I asked him if he wanted to come back to Montvelatte for a while,' Rafe continued, 'but he said his mother needed him there. He might bring her in a while, when she's accepted it more.'

'Of course,' she said, his words washing over her, meaningless in the minefield that was her mind. And then, because she might never know, she asked, 'Rafe?'

'Yes?'

'What caused Yannis's father's death?'

'It was a stroke. He had a history of them, starting about ten years back.'

She rubbed her forehead with one hand. It made no sense. How could Yannis hold her responsible for something like that? 'What triggered them off?'

'Money troubles, apparently. The family lost a fortune. His father had big plans to join forces with the de Santo shipping family. They'd brokered a deal that would see the Markides family one of the strongest shipping dynasties in the world.'

'And it went wrong?'

'Horribly wrong. Part of the deal, apparently, was that Yannis would marry Elena de Santo. It was all arranged.'

'He was going to be married?' Hadn't Sienna hinted at something in his past? 'I didn't know.'

'Not many people did. It was all supposed to be announced on his twenty-first birthday. That was the intention, anyway.'

Ice ran through her veins. His twenty-first. *Thirteen years ago.* The same time… Please, God, no. It couldn't be. She whispered into the phone, 'What happened?'

'Apparently, there was talk of him having an affair— a woman was seen leaving his room the night before the intended betrothal. The engagement never got announced, and the deal fell through. Meanwhile, Yannis's father had everything riding on the deal. He'd already severed contact with his former business partners and was relying on the wedding going ahead. It almost destroyed the family financially. Yannis has been slogging his guts out ever since, trying to make up for it.'

She forced the words through trembling lips. 'Who was the woman?'

'He never said.'

He didn't have to. Someone had seen her leaving his room. Her eyes had been too filled with tears to see anything clearly. She'd stumbled back to her room, her hands in front of her face, her stupid teenage heart breaking.

And she'd been worried for herself, distraught at her humiliation, never giving a thought to the ramifications, never having any idea what she'd cost him.

She let her brother say goodbye, sending her love, her numb mind slashed back into agony with the repercussions of her foolish act of love.

Her reckless actions had not only cost him a wife. She'd cost his family millions. And now she'd cost him his father.

No wonder he hated her!

CHAPTER TWELVE

SUNSET in Hawaii was spectacular, the setting sun turning clouds of cotton wool a thousand shades of pink, and sending silver-red ribbons dancing over the sea. And nowhere was it more spectacular, Marietta thought, than viewed from the beach, with sandals in one hand, bare feet splashing through the shallows, and the sunset framed on one side by the silhouette of a palm on the shore.

It was her favourite time of day, one she too often missed with the gallery's late opening hours, but even after two months in Honolulu, she never grew tired of it. While always spectacular, it was different too, every single time.

She stopped in the shallows near where some children were playing and looked out to sea, past a stoic line of surfers still waiting for that perfect wave and refusing to give in to the failing light, past the sleek white lines of the cruise ship heading into port, to the horizon beyond. Somewhere behind her someone was strumming a ukulele and making it sing, and she sighed for the beauty of the world in which she lived.

She had a lot to be thankful for. The gallery was going well, the early influx of new customers settling into a steadily building trade, helped once again by Duke Kameāloha, who had taken to visiting the gallery on a regular basis and had been pictured wearing pieces of her work. Xavier was in his element dealing with his new clientele, and looked more like his normal self than he had in months, his decision to make the move into Honolulu fully vindicated.

And by all accounts Sienna's pregnancy was progressing well, with the prospect of a couple of new royals in the Montvelatte line-up in just a few short months.

It was all good.

And as for this ache she felt sometimes when she thought about a dark-haired man who was better looking than any man had a right to be—that would fade, she was sure of it. Time was supposed to be a great healer, after all.

She just needed more of it.

The children disappeared, the cruise boat had long gone, and the surfers gave up and paddled to shore one by one as the horizon faded, eaten up as sea and sky became one.

She sighed as she splashed back along the way she had come, feeling both awed and inspired by the shifting light show. Life was good. Just witnessing a sunset like that was a blessing.

She was almost ready to leave the beach and cross the road to her apartment block where she now had a modern apartment overlooking the water, when she saw someone coming the other way along the shore, someone tall and broad, whose olive-skinned face glowed in the moonlight. And for one moment, just one insane moment that sent a pulse of electricity jagging through her, she thought it was him.

And just when she thought she'd been mad to think it, he spoke. 'Hello, Marietta.'

She stopped there in the shallows as he closed the distance between them, with the waves sucking at her feet not the only force suddenly turning her hold on the world unsteady. 'Yannis?'

Even in the darkness she could see he looked different. His hair curled a little more at his neck, his features were less drawn. Even his clothes, the untucked casual shirt and folded-up cotton pants, their bottoms dark where the shallow waves had caught him, looked different.

'It took me a while to find you. You've moved.'

She shrugged. 'The house was too big.' Too big and too filled with memories, too empty without him. 'I found an apartment down here. It looks over the sea and I can walk to work. The best of both worlds.' Her words trailed away, sucked into the night, and he made no attempt to catch them, just kept looking at her, making her ask over and over again in her head what he was doing and why he was here.

'So,' he said at last, 'how are you?'

'Good! The gallery is doing well. Xavier is delighted. He thinks that—'

'No,' he said, with a quiet authority that stopped her in her tracks. 'I asked how *you* were doing?'

She nodded, still wondering whether he meant how

she'd been doing before he'd appeared out of the night, or right now, faced with seeing him again, two utterly different things. Thrown right off balance would have been the answer to the latter.

She chose to answer the former. 'Okay,' she said, with more than a grain of truth. Maybe her life now lacked the fireworks of the first few days here with Yannis, but that wasn't necessarily a bad thing, given the outcome. And she'd settled into life and work here in Honolulu, accepting the humidity was the price you paid for living in a tropical paradise like this one. 'Yeah, I'm okay. How about you?'

He shrugged, his hands in his pockets. 'Good. I've been on Montvelatte the last couple of weeks, visiting Rafe and Sienna. I took my mother back. It's been years since she's been there. Did Rafe tell you?'

Marietta shook her head, frowning. Rafe had spoken to her just a couple of nights ago, but he'd said nothing about having visitors, let alone made mention of Yannis. 'How is your mother?' Marietta asked. 'I heard…' She licked her lips, knowing there was no easy way to say it. Knowing how he felt about what she'd done. Knowing she had more right than ever now to utter the two little words—*I'm sorry*—that had turned him so crazy with anger the last time they'd been together. Had he come for an apology? The apology he thought she owed him? 'I heard about your father.'

He heaved in a breath and let it out, looking sightlessly over the ceaseless sea before turning back to her. 'Do you mind if we walk together?'

She shook her head, and they headed back up the beach. 'What are you doing in Hawaii?' she asked. *Why are you here?*

'A client,' he said, and the pieces settled into some kind of pattern in her head. Something else had brought him here. He was probably just looking her up because her big brother had expected him to.

'So Rafe asked you to check up on me?'

'Did I say that?'

'No, but—'

'Then why assume it?' He looked around the rapidly emptying beach. 'Are you cold?'

With him next to her? He had to be kidding? 'No.'

'Then can we sit a while?'

She was about to say they could sit in her apartment, but she wasn't sure she wanted him there. She'd moved from the Kahala house not only because it was too big, but because it was filled with memories of Yannis. In the kitchen, in the entry hall, and the bedroom he'd long since vacated, and even on the beach.

No. She didn't need memories of Yannis cluttering up her apartment once he had decided to disappear again. And so they sat in the still-warm sand, peering into the dark moonlit night and listening to the white foam edge of the surf dance along the shore, half of her wishing he'd never come back, the other half strangely hoping—a hope that she knew could never come true.

And even just sitting and watching and listening to the waves, not talking, not even looking at each other, she felt his heat and his power in every fibre of her being. She didn't want to feel him now, not after all that had happened. But denying his impact on her was like trying to deny the sunset.

And who could deny the sunset? Not her. But now it was night, the sunset gone, and the weight of the unsaid dragged heavy upon her soul. She looked across at him, resting back on his elbows as he looked out to sea, and even just one glance at his profile shifted something in her soul. Something she knew instinctively no amount of time would eradicate.

'Yannis?'

He rolled his head towards her, looking more relaxed than ever. 'Yes?'

'Rafe told me about Elena. About your planned engagement.'

His eyes widened and he resettled his weight on his arms, but he said nothing.

'He told me that the wedding was called off because someone thought you were having an affair, that a woman had been seen leaving your room.'

He blinked, slowly, his dark eyes unreadable in the twilight apart from the occasional reflection from the lights, enough to know that they never left her.

'Rafe didn't know who, but that was me, wasn't it? Someone spotted me. And they assumed the worst, that you were having an affair. All because of my stupid teenage crush.'

He sat up suddenly, brushing the sand from his elbows and resting them on his knees.

'It doesn't matter.'

'Oh, but it does.' She bit her lip, wanting to continue without giving too much of herself away. But the weight of knowing the damage she'd done with her reckless act pressed down on her resolve and with it her tear ducts. A single tear squeezed out. 'I couldn't work out why you were so angry towards me before, but finally it made sense.' She paused. 'It was me, wasn't it? You'd thrown me out, you'd made sure nothing happened, and still you were held accountable.'

He shook his head. 'It wasn't like that.'

'But the result was the same! The wedding was called off. The deal between the families in tatters.'

He couldn't deny the truth of that. It had been an ugly scene—the first of many—when he'd been dragged in to answer for his sins, the sound of Elena's father accusing, the shouts of his own father defending, knowing what was on the line and trying desperately to shore up his position before he lost everything.

And then his father had asked Yannis, in one final desperate appeal against the hearsay evidence that was going to pull him down, to swear before God that he hadn't been with another woman and that he was free to marry Elena…

'Did you love her?'

He was so deep in memories, the question so left-field, that he had to look at her to work out who she was talking about.'

'Who? Elena?'

'Who else? You were going to marry her.' And he almost laughed with the absurdity of it.

'I never loved her. I didn't even know her that well. She was tall and beautiful and would have looked good on anyone's arm, but no. I never loved her.'

'And you didn't marry her. And it destroyed your family.' She looked back out to sea, tears blurring her vision as she remembered another time when she'd tried to say she was sorry, and she remembered how that ended. 'And this time, when I say I'm sorry, I really am. I'm sorry, Yannis. Sorry I did that to you and to your family. I'm sorry for what it cost your father.'

She stood suddenly, unable to sit any longer, not with the weight of the guilt she bore. She swiped at her eyes, clearing away tears she'd thought she'd long forgotten. 'Thanks for looking me up. It was great to catch up.'

He was up and alongside her in a heartbeat. 'You think I'm leaving now?'

She sniffed. 'Do we have anything else to talk about?'

'How about how much I need to apologise to you.'

'You don't have to apologise for throwing me out. I know I made a mess of everything. It was a stupid thing for me to do. What else could you do?' She turned to walk away, but he stopped her with one hand to her arm.

'No! Listen to me!' And his voice held a note so compelling that she nodded and faced him again.

He dragged in air. He'd been away a long time, a long time thinking it all through, and yet it was only tonight that the final piece had fallen into place. How fitting that that might finally happen when he was here, with Marietta once again.

'My father had a grand plan. He wanted to transform

the Markides name into a huge name in shipping, and he had an ally—a shipping magnate with a daughter, who had no thought to business and even less care who she married. He thought if he married her to someone who would look after the business, it would solve everything. Meanwhile, my father could see an opportunity to expand his own interests. He courted this man like one would court a wife, with promises and gifts and guarantees.

'The one thing they forgot was to tell me. I learned about it the afternoon before my twenty-first birthday. It was all planned, they told me. The announcement would be made and our families would reap the benefits for generations.'

'And then I came to your room.'

He smiled then, if you could call it that. 'I didn't hear you come in. I can't believe I woke at all that night. Unable to change my father's mind, I raided his bar, choosing the whisky, the one thing I knew he hated the most. I have no idea how much I drank, but I was dead to the world until you arrived. And even then I didn't think it was you.'

'You didn't know it was me?'

'I should have. But I'd drunk more than my share. I came to, thinking my father and his crony had planned to bring the honeymoon forward. I thought they'd sent Elena, and I got angry and decided I wouldn't take it lying down. That I would be the one to do the taking. And then, to my horror, I discovered it was you.'

'To your horror?'

'Don't you see? I was angry. Not with you, but with who I assumed was in my bed. The horror came when I realised that it wasn't Elena under me but you, when you deserved so much more…'

His words sounded so fluid, and yet still the memory of that night ground against her senses, metal scraping against metal. 'And yet you still threw me out.'

'How could I let you stay when I knew I was to become engaged to another the very next night?'

'Why didn't you tell me? Did you have to be so heartless?'

He turned away, remembering the night and his feelings. Ashamed of them. 'I had to throw you out.'

'But why?'

'Don't you understand? Because I knew I could never have you, not if I was to marry Elena. But I wanted you so much. And you were there, naked in my bed. And for one bleary moment I thought I could have you, and still marry Elena, and nobody would know.'

'I would have known.'

'And me. Which is why I couldn't do it. I had to get you out of there before I made things worse. Before I spoiled you for anyone else.'

The waves rolled in and whooshed out, the wind rustled the palm leaves high above them, and beyond that intruded the sound of the city, with traffic noises and voices and laughter. But right now, right here, it was Yannis's words that consumed her senses.

'Why would that matter?'

'Because you were too perfect to be spoiled.'

His words filtered down, trying to find a place to settle in the murkiness of memories and their allotted interpretation. Too perfect? He'd thought she was too perfect?

'But you made me feel that it was all my fault. That you hated me because of what I'd done.'

'I did.' He shook his head. 'At least I thought I did. I had to blame someone. You were the one thing that linked me to a marriage that I didn't want and the failure of my family's fortune. You tied both strands together. And you were guilt and want and need all rolled into one ready excuse. It was more comfortable to blame you than me. I knew you'd never want me, not after what I'd done to you, so it all made sense. I might as well hate you if you were going to hate me.'

'So you decided to hate me.' She clutched her arms around her, not knowing what to believe, not understanding what it all meant. Only knowing that it was too much to take in. Too much to accept. 'And is that why you held me responsible for your father's illness? Is that why you practically blamed me for your father's death?'

She veered blindly away across the sand, not caring about direction, only knowing that she had to get away. How could he do this to her—and why?—after all he'd put her through?

But he caught her and spun her into his arms. 'I was wrong! I blamed you for so many, many things. Because I didn't want to face up to the blame myself. Those things were my responsibility, my onus to bear. And only tonight have I realised that fact.

'When it became known that someone had seen a

woman—you—leaving my room, and everything was set to blow up in my father's face, he called me into a meeting with him and Elena's father, a last-ditch effort to save the deal. He asked me to swear before God that it was all lies. That I hadn't been with another woman and that I had done nothing that might threaten my marriage to Elena.' He dragged in a breath. 'It should have been easy to deny it.'

'But you didn't.'

He turned his gaze to look down on her. He shook his head. 'I didn't. I told him there had been a woman. I flaunted it in his face, although I never told him who.'

He dropped to his knees on the sand, his hands locked together. 'I made that decision. I chose to disobey him. And it was easier to blame you for what happened afterwards because I knew you would hate me anyway.' He paused. 'And it was easier than blaming myself.'

She reached out a reluctant hand, touching his shoulder tentatively with her fingertips, wanting to believe his words, to trust him, but still with too much holding her back. 'You told me you'd thrown me out of bed because I was a virgin. That wasn't true. And yet I believed you at the time. That's why I couldn't let you make love to me in Montvelatte the night of the wedding. I was scared. Scared of the act itself, but more scared of what you would think of me.'

His fingers caught hers at his shoulder and brought them to his mouth, squeezing his lips to them. 'How could I give you a reason that you would understand?'

'I know that, and yet, when we did finally make love,

you made out like it was the worst thing in the world, like you'd really meant it.'

'I hurt you,' he said. 'I'd hurt you enough. I should have known. I'm sorry. It should have been better.'

She let herself drop back down on the sand alongside him, letting him pick up her hand and weave her fingers around his own. She looked out to the dark sea, its ridges highlighted by the moon, its endless waves rolling into the shore and crashing in a line of foam.

How could that world look so unchanged when inside her there'd been a seismic shift of such massive proportions? He'd explained what he'd done and why. He'd told her that he'd wronged her. He'd told her he was sorry.

Yannis, her Yannis, had told her he was sorry. And under the tropical moon and the gentle sway of palms, she believed him.

'So how could it be better?' she asked, and the hand around hers momentarily stilled before he looked across at her, a question clouding his face, though she noticed his dark eyes were already tinged with desire.

'Believe me, it could be much better.'

Oh, my. She swallowed and turned away, her mouth suddenly dry at the prospect. But his hand hauled her back, and she went to him willingly, the look in his eyes burning into her soul.

'I have no right to ask this of you after everything that I've done to you and accused you of,' he said, hesitating, 'but is there a chance that you might one day forgive me so that we might start again?'

A heart that had been sluggish for too long and too wary with it suddenly kicked into life. 'You want my forgiveness?'

'Please.'

'And you want the chance to start again?'

'If you can see your way clear.'

And still self-preservation ruled that his declaration wasn't enough. 'But why? What's changed this time? How can I be sure that you won't find some other reason to reject me?'

'Because I love you.'

The world stopped. Or was it just her heart? 'What did you say?'

'I love you. I only wish it hadn't taken me so long to realise it.'

Tears welled up in her eyes. Tears of happiness that wouldn't be stopped, no matter how much she swiped them clear.

He frowned, looking concerned. 'You're crying.'

'I'm happy,' she said, swiping at her cheek again. 'I just never believed you'd ever say that.'

'Believe it. I love you, Marietta. And if one thing being away from you has taught me, I can't live without you. I have to be with you, every day, every night. Please say you'll give me another chance.'

And he looked at her so earnestly that she felt his words resonate deep inside, in a place that had been waiting for this one special moment for what seemed like for ever. She wrapped her hands around his and leaned in close to him. 'I think I was born to love you,

Yannis Markides. I had no choice then, and I have no choice now. I love you with all my heart and soul.'

And her heart kicked over with the smile she received in return, a smile that sent warmth radiating right through her. 'So you'll give me one more chance?'

'On one condition,' she warned. 'Only if you show me how it could be better.'

He didn't disappoint. This time they went back to her apartment, and he made love to her, with his hands, with his body, with his tongue. He kissed away the hurt of bad times, he showed her how much he loved her, and then he showed her how good it could be. She responded in kind, proving what a good student she was, luxuriating in his body, drinking him in through her very pores. And this time, when ecstasy sent them soaring into the abyss, their souls went together, united as one.

Evening turned to night. Night became dawn, and morning turned bright with the new sun and a brand new day. The first day for them together.

Through it all she showed him how much she loved him, and he showed her how much he loved her. And when finally they drifted towards sleep, fully sated, replete, she leaned up drowsily to kiss his lips. 'I love you, Yannis,' she murmured, 'so much.'

He cradled her closer as he returned the kiss, knowing that tonight he had been given the gift of love, a gift he would cherish for ever. 'I am honoured, my princess,' he told her, kissing the tip of her nose and then her chin. 'And I will love you for ever.'

EPILOGUE

BELLS rang out in towers from Velatte City to the tiniest village, women decked buildings and donkeys and even themselves with garlands of flowers, and the mood was festive. The people of Montvelatte were celebrating, and with good cause.

Prince Luca and Princess Annabella had put in an appearance right on time, and the royal twins were already winning hearts, the first pictures cut out of the local papers and pinned to walls all over the island.

Inside the Castello, things were no less exciting, the royal babies turning palace life upside down, but they brought with them so much joy that nobody complained. And it wasn't just that the continuing existence of the royal line had been assured. New life had been breathed into the principality by Prince Raphael and Princess Sienna over the last few months, and it showed on the faces of everyone, from the loftiest employee whose job had been assured by Rafe's financial rescue package, to the youngest school child, thrilled to receive a visit from the new princess.

Marietta and Yannis were there to celebrate the new additions to the family. And to pass on some good news of their own when the time was right.

It was a joyful reunion, the addition of the two new royals making it extra special. 'Which one do you like the most?' asked Sienna before dinner, and Marietta couldn't choose between them—Annabella with her dark lashes and hair, or Luca with his plump cheeks and cupid's bow mouth. 'They're both so beautiful,' she said, unable to decide. 'I adore them both.' And Sienna laughed and said she felt the same way, picking up Luca as he squawked into wakefulness.

'How are things in Honolulu going?' Sienna asked as Marietta similarly scooped up Annabella from her crib.

'Wonderful,' said Marietta without having to think about it. She pressed a kiss to the baby's soft downy hair. 'Business is great. The gallery is going well and…'

'And?'

And Yannis was there every other week.

'And it's good,' she said, with a secret smile.

'Is that so?' Sienna asked, with a smile of her own. 'That is good.'

The two men joined them then, Rafe immediately going to his wife's side and wrapping his arm around her, kissing her before smiling down at the baby squirming in her arms.

Yannis joined Marietta, his hand at her shoulder, his fingertips stroking her neck as he looked down at the infant in her arms.

'Look at her. She's so beautiful, Yannis.'

And he touched his free hand to the infant's head and smiled. 'She is. Congratulations to you both.'

He looked up to see both Sienna and Rafe studying him. Or rather, studying what his other hand was doing at Marietta's neck. They looked at each other briefly before Sienna said, 'We were actually wondering if we were the only ones around here with good news.'

And it was Yannis's turn to exchange glances with Marietta. 'Did you tell her?'

Marietta smiled. 'I think she might have guessed.'

And Sienna laughed, the baby still in her arms. 'Come on. Spill!'

Yannis kissed the woman he loved and pulled her close. 'In that case, you can be the first to know that Marietta has very kindly agreed to become my wife.'

'I knew it!' Sienna cried, handing her baby to its father so she could rush over and hug them both. 'Congratulations. I'm so happy for you.'

Annabella ended up with Yannis so Sienna could hug her sister-in-law properly, and the two women spun off in a whirl of excitement.

It was minutes later that they looked up and noticed. Rafe and Yannis were standing next to each other talking, a tiny dark-haired bundle cradled somewhat awkwardly, but nonetheless seemingly contentedly, in their arms.

'Oh, my,' said Marietta, transfixed by the vision of Yannis, her powerful Yannis, holding such a tiny baby with such tender care. 'I had no idea.'

Sienna followed her gaze and smiled. 'I know. That's the best bit. Being in love just keeps on getting better and better.'

And she was right.

MILLS & BOON
MODERN™
On sale 21st August 2009

MARCHESE'S FORGOTTEN BRIDE
by Michelle Reid

Alessandro Marchese's forgotten Cassie and their twins, but as his memory returns, he plans to complete the picture and take Cassie as his bride!

POWERFUL GREEK, UNWORLDLY WIFE
by Sarah Morgan

When scandal threatened Millie's perfect life with Leandro, she ran. Now Leandro is demanding she come home…

KYRIAKIS'S INNOCENT MISTRESS
by Diana Hamilton

Dimitri wants revenge and seduces his father's mistress. But innocent Bonnie is really only the hired help. Too late he discovers she was a virgin!

SPANISH ARISTOCRAT, FORCED BRIDE
by India Grey

After one night with playboy Tristan, Lily discovers she's pregnant. Duty demands they marry and she'll be expected to fulfil his *every* need…

THE COSTANZO BABY SECRET
by Catherine Spencer

Maeve's accident destroyed her memories of her husband and baby son. To reawaken his wife Dario will seduce her…

Available at WHSmith, Tesco, ASDA, Eason and all good bookshops
www.millsandboon.co.uk

0809/01b

MILLS & BOON
MODERN
On sale 4th September 2009

THE BRAZILIAN MILLIONAIRE'S LOVE-CHILD
by Anne Mather

Three years after he took her virginity, Isobel meets
Brazilian millionaire Alejandro again. Gorgeous but
scarred, he wants his child...

THE VIRGIN SECRETARY'S IMPOSSIBLE BOSS
by Carole Mortimer

Billionaire Linus relishes the chance to undo Andrea's buttoned-
up exterior. Snowbound in Scotland, how can Andi resist?

RICH, RUTHLESS AND SECRETLY ROYAL
by Robyn Donald

Prince Kelt knows the responsibility a title brings, so keeps his
position hidden. Hani has never known a man like Kelt, but he's
holding a secret...one almost as dark as her own!

KEPT FOR HER BABY
by Kate Walker

Lucy will do anything for her baby – even return to her husband.
Ricardo branded his bride a gold-digger and he'll keep Lucy
captive until she proves herself a worthy wife...

THE MEDITERRANEAN'S WIFE BY CONTRACT
by Kathryn Ross

Carrie is godmother to Andreas's orphaned baby niece but
Andreas is determined to keep her. He's offering her a
deal she can't refuse – marriage!

Available at WHSmith, Tesco, ASDA, Eason and all good bookshops
www.millsandboon.co.uk

RUGBY_GEN

INTERNATIONAL BILLIONAIRES

*From rich tycoons to royal playboys –
they're red-hot and ruthless*

COLLECT ALL 8 VOLUMES AND COMPLETE THE SET!

Available February 2009

Win
A LUXURY RUGBY
WEEKEND!

see inside books for details

MILLS & BOON
MODERN
www.millsandboon.co.uk

THESE HOT-BLOODED TYCOONS ARE INTENT ON TAKING A BRIDE!

Featuring three gorgeous Greeks in:

The Greek's Chosen Wife
Lynne Graham

Bought by the Greek Tycoon
by Jacqueline Baird

The Greek's Forbidden Bride
by Cathy Williams

Available 17th July 2009

www.millsandboon.co.uk

Rich, successful and gorgeous...

These Australian men clearly need wives!

Featuring:

THE WEALTHY AUSTRALIAN'S PROPOSAL
by Margaret Way

THE BILLIONAIRE CLAIMS HIS WIFE
by Amy Andrews

INHERITED BY THE BILLIONAIRE
by Jennie Adams

Available 21st August 2009

WEB/M&B/RTL

™ MILLS & BOON ®

www.millsandboon.co.uk

◉ All the latest titles

◉ Free online reads

◉ Irresistible special offers

And there's more...

◉ Missed a book? Buy from our huge discounted backlist

◉ Sign up to our FREE monthly eNewsletter

◉ eBooks available now

◉ More about your favourite authors

◉ Great competitions

Make sure you visit today!

www.millsandboon.co.uk

2 FREE BOOKS
AND A SURPRISE GIFT

We would like to take this opportunity to thank you for reading this Mills & Boon® book by offering you the chance to take TWO more specially selected titles from the Modern™ series absolutely FREE! We're also making this offer to introduce you to the benefits of the Mills & Boon® Book Club™—

- **FREE home delivery**
- **FREE gifts and competitions**
- **FREE monthly Newsletter**
- **Exclusive Mills & Boon Book Club offers**
- **Books available before they're in the shops**

Accepting these FREE books and gift places you under no obligation to buy, you may cancel at any time, even after receiving your free books. Simply complete your details below and return the entire page to the address below. You don't even need a stamp!

YES Please send me 2 free Modern books and a surprise gift. I understand that unless you hear from me, I will receive 4 superb new titles every month for just £3.19 each, postage and packing free. I am under no obligation to purchase any books and may cancel my subscription at any time. The free books and gift will be mine to keep in any case.

Ms/Mrs/Miss/Mr_____ initials _____

Surname _____

address _____

_____

_____ postcode _____

Send this whole page to: Mills & Boon Book Club, Free Book Offer, FREEPOST NAT 10298, Richmond, TW9 1BR

Offer valid in UK only and is not available to current Mills & Boon Book Club subscribers to this series. Overseas and Eire please write for details.. We reserve the right to refuse an application and applicants must be aged 18 years or over. Only one application per household. Terms and prices subject to change without notice. Offer expires 31st October 2009. As a result of this application, you may receive offers from Harlequin Mills & Boon and other carefully selected companies. If you would prefer not to share in this opportunity please write to The Data Manager, PO Box 676, Richmond, TW9 1WU.

Mills & Boon® is a registered trademark owned by Harlequin Mills & Boon Limited.
Modern™ is being used as a trademark. The Mills & Boon® Book Club™ is being used as a trademark.